Everything Turns Out Just Fine

Peter Tarnofsky

Also by Peter Tarnofsky:

They All Die At The End
Timestand
Benny Baker

www.petertarnofsky.co.uk

Cover photograph of St Ives, Cornwall by the author.
Crayon-effect sun drawn by the author.

Everything Turns Out Just Fine

Peter Tarnofsky

Many thanks are due to the following people who pre-ordered this book before I had even finished writing it. Knowing that readers are out there, eagerly anticipating, is a wonderful incentive. Maybe this book wouldn't be as good otherwise.
Let's assume that.

In no particular order (other than family first):
Mum and Dad, Sarah and Peter Nickson, Ivy Charters, Jonathan Charters,
Keith Goldstein, Kim & Ian, The Simons Family, Mike & Joyce Lewins, casey kitten,
Mina Kupfermann, Karen Silver, Pete & Nobuko Weitz, Katy Weitz, Susy Weitz,
The Garcia Family, Justin Presser, Sammy and Elliott Myers,
Andrew and Ruth Burns, Kampfbeagles, Jürgen & Justin, Sherard and Sheila Wilson,
Oliver Lewis, The Heeks Family, Ian Shine, Pamela and Adrian Jacobs,
James Rokos, Michele Galla, Zac Grant, The Lill Family, Alastair Tatton,
T. Michael Pitt, Megan Griffiths, Cally Phillips, E C Daley, Al and Carol Perlman,
Peter Stern, The Edmonds, Eugene Magee, Pam Lewis, Alex the Wild, Lyrania,
Grayson Bowler, Stuart Lofthouse, J Alexander D Atkins, Weasel

First published in Great Britain in 2013.

First edition.

Copyright © Peter Tarnofsky 2013

The moral right of the author has been asserted, although the author doesn't entirely know what that means but is sure that this ignorance doesn't affect his right to assert.

ISBN 978 1 291 46324 8

to all those who wondered
why the other book had to be quite so dark –
here's one that's all smiles (mostly)

Contents

Nobody Died

Nobody died, although one person inadvisedly issued a death threat and another certainly wished that the ground would swallow him.

The death threat sounded like this: "You know I could probably find someone who could have you killed." Gabriel was disappointed. Bob wasn't going to do it himself – hell, he wasn't even going to organise it himself. He was going to staff out arranging the outsourcing of the killing – he was keeping himself so far removed from the action that even putting him into the sentence made the grammar uncomfortable.

But Gabriel told Bob that the call was being recorded for training purposes and Bob gave a little silence then a little laugh and they didn't return to the subject. Well, a bit later, Gabriel explained what would probably happen if he died; and they both agreed that it would be a Bad Thing and that was that.

Bob was sure that it was all Phil's fault which, technically, it was. Phil thought that Gabriel was behaving badly and that it was tantamount to theft. Gabriel felt that if people like Bob were going to get fancy-pants lawyers to draw up ghastly, over-long and impenetrable contracts then it was only fair that they'd get spanked by it themselves once in a while.

The triangle of blame wasn't helping anyone. Except Gabriel – he didn't really care whose fault it was as long as no one could do anything about it.

Phil had been with Bob's company since Day Three. This was not, of course, the third day of the company but the beginning of the third phase, according to the word of Bob. Phil's most recent appraisal from his most recent boss had the same two entries in 'areas for improvement' as all the previous appraisals.

> *1. Phil should strive to be an ambassador for the global corporate directives and motivate his team to drive the changes.*

Phil read that sentence twice before looking up at his most recent boss, curiously called Louise just like her predecessor, and giving her his standard raised-eyebrow look of frustration. Just engage with the memos, Phil. Just respect the company line, Phil. Just stop mocking the wording, Phil. This stuff works, Phil. Bob's running a multi-billion dollar company, Phil, and you're not – so maybe consider that he knows more about it than you do.

> *2. Phil must display more trust in his team and learn to delegate so that he may focus on his core responsibilities.*

You think I'm micro-managing, Louise? I know you're micro-managing, Phil. Monitor, delegate, manage, advise but let them get on with their jobs and then you can get on with yours. I do get on with my job, Louise. I get things done, Louise. And if you want me to trust my team, how about involving me in recruitment? Then I might actually get some underlings that I could trust with the work, Louise. I'd like to recommend you for promotion, Phil, but you've got two big areas for improvement that need addressing first. You're putting me in a Catch-22, Louise. No, Phil, you've just got two areas to catch-up on.

Phil's eyebrows nearly raised but he held them back. He had stock options, which was more than Louise or Louise had. They came and went, he just had to ride it out.

And in the small hours of Sunday morning, when it was quiet, when Phil could concentrate, he completed his testing of the system changes. And he found, with a snort of grudging respect, that they had done a good job after all. And the system flowed and processed and allowed the data to burble happily through as his fictitious customers bought fictitious ebooks to read on their fictitious ebook readers.

And, just for old time's sake, he put the last test through, the one where you put in the smallest possible number of sales (one copy – Failed Author's Zero was tested elsewhere) and then the largest possible number of sales (one shy of a billion).

And on the way home, he couldn't shake off the anxiety that there had been an 'L' for 'live', not a 'Q' for 'quality-assurance test', in the corner of the screen. No, *he'd* never be that stupid but clearly that would be another reason why someone as senior as him, someone with his level of clearance and access and Power, shouldn't be running tests because Accidents Will Happen.

It was accidental, at first, when Gabriel started the Rhyming Thing. Bob said that they should talk face-to-face and Gabriel said the phone was fine and Bob said he could send a car to pick Gabriel up and Gabriel said, "I could just drive in mine". Bob would have let that go, it happens all the time, but then Gabriel suggested discussing things over a bottle of wine and that he wasn't trying to act like a swine and that if Bob made a sensible offer he wouldn't decline – hell, he'd probably sign, yes, on the dotted line.

And Bob nearly raised his voice and nearly said, "listen here, sunshine" but instead stayed calm and fired back with "enough of your juice, Dr Seuss" which he thought was pretty good under the circumstances, until Gabriel pointed out that 'Seuss' should rhyme with 'voice' since it's a Germanic name and Bob fired back that almost no one in the English-speaking world pronounced it like that. And Gabriel asked if Bob had got where he was in life by following all the mistakes that other people made and Bob still didn't raise his voice but merely said that they seemed to have Gone Off On A Tangent.

But we're getting ahead of ourselves. The Rhyming Thing happened before the Death Threat but they both happened after Bob's phone rang while inside the x-ray machine, which caused a brief fracas while men in fluorescent vests spoke urgently and seriously to men in camouflage uniform. At least Bob did not prolong the situation by demanding that he be allowed to answer it.

Gabriel's phone rang while he was typing his PIN into the cashpoint machine. He wasn't sure if he would be getting any cash or not. He'd have to check his balance first.

Bob took his seat – reasonably good view, but then he was only a third-tier sponsor, good enough to get the brand name on the posters (without the logo), good enough to get a fistful of tickets to split between himself and competition winners, but not good enough for trackside, for glad-handing the winners, for getting picked out by the cameras in three-dimensional high-definition.

Louise Glover said, "I think you need to talk to Louise Phelps. I don't work in that department. Shall I call her for you? Is there anything else I can help you with today?"

No one was supposed to call Bob today, not unless it was Really Important. His current wife and his new children were with him. Everyone else could wait. Everyone else had been told. But there was the message, the little symbol on the shiny screen nagging away at him. He had to know.

"How much?" was a question that Bob, Gabriel, both Louises and Phil asked that morning. Bob and the Louises had their turn at answering it. Every conversation involved either the phrase "billion, yes, with a 'b'" or "not million, *billion*".

"So *now* you'll speak to me. I tried to speak to you last year," said Gabriel, early in his conversation with Bob. "They fobbed me off."

"I run a multi-billion dollar business," said Bob. "I can't deal with the nickel and dime stuff."

"Mr Tucker, that's a little patronising, don't you think?"

"I apologise."

"Thank you. Believe it or not, an apology was all I wanted in the end," said Gabriel.

"I'm sorry," said Phil when Louise had explained what he had done and he finally believed her. "It was an accident. I was under a lot of pressure."

"It wouldn't have happened if you'd delegated, Phil," said Louise.

"I couldn't be sure they would do it right."

"That's what delegating *is*, Phil. It's trusting your team to do it right. How many mistakes did you find?"

"The system worked perfectly. But I couldn't know that unless I tested it myself."

"Had your team tested it themselves, Phil?"

"Yes. But..."

"So was more than one person responsible, Phil? What has been on your appraisal every year since goodness knows when, Phil?"

"Okay, I know, I need to delegate and manage and monitor and whatever else it is but..."

"Actually, you don't, Phil. Not any more, Phil," said Louise Phelps because Louise Glover had told her to.

"I can't," said Gabriel, because this is a little later in his conversation with Bob and he's sticking to his guns that it's out of his hands now that it's fallen in his lap. Only, he's an author so he wouldn't use three clichés like that in the same sentence. Oh, we haven't had the Death Threat yet but the Rhyming Thing has happened.

"Why not?" asked Bob, chuckling. The Feeling Insulted by the Rhyming Thing has passed.

"Because, if I did, you could sue me for breach of contract," said Gabriel, also chuckling.

"I don't think I'd do that," said Bob, no longer chuckling.

"I'd be uncomfortable breaking the terms," said Gabriel. "After all, I'm happy with the agreement and I don't think you can unilaterally make alterations now."

The crowd roared its approval as the favourite, the local boy, the chat-show-friendly athlete, the poster-boy face of whichever sports apparel,

lolloped across the line. Bob held out his hand for
quiet, a reflexive gesture from a man too used to
control to realise the limits of his power.

"I'm sorry, did you say something?" asked
Gabriel. He was reclining on his sofa, television
showing him the sport, tablet computer providing
the irreverent commentary, phone giving the slightly
out-of-synch crowd roar. "Are you at the games?
Give me a wave if the camera comes your way."

"I don't think so," said Bob, standing up, moving
towards the aisle, dodging the discarded paper cups,
handbags, umbrellas. He didn't give even a
backwards glance to his family. But they didn't look
up when he wandered off either. The global head of
a multi-billion dollar business couldn't always give
his family Uninterrupted Face-Time.

"That's you!" cried Gabriel. "I can see you on the
TV."

Bob glanced up at the screen proudly straddling
the top of the stands and saw himself, on the phone,
walking away from the action. Probably some minor
reality-television starlet in the row behind, he
thought. He wouldn't recognise her anyway.

"Listen," he said, once he had reached the
relative quiet of the corridor. "I know you think
you're in a position of power. But you're not.
Money gained in error is money that must be
returned. Otherwise it's just theft. And it sounds
like you're warming up for a bit of extortion and
that's never going to play well in court."

"I know," said Gabriel.

"So you were just yanking my chain?" asked Bob, the smile nearly returning, the chuckle ready in the throat.

"Not at all," said Gabriel. "I know all that stuff about money gained in error. I used phrases like that myself last year, with your charming staff. Your computer system snarled up and forgot to charge for forty-three copies of my ebook. So I didn't get my royalty. And it was explained to me, perfectly clearly, hang on, I've got the email here... right... in the event of any system error, software error, user error, agent error, banking error, accounting error or any other error..."

"I get the idea," said Bob.

"I know, it does go on a bit. Pay them by the word, do you? Frankly, I don't know why they list so many types of error if they're going to stick 'Any Other Error' on the end."

"Yeah. Ha ha."

"Okay. So, to cut a long story short..."

"I think it's a bit late for that now."

"No monies are to be paid by way of recompense, compensation, reward, penalty, fee or fine."

"That's from us to you," said Bob. Something a bit lunchy was bubbling up from his stomach.

"It doesn't say that," said Gabriel. "So I reckon it's very clear that I am required to not reimburse you."

"Okay, so you're not required to reimburse us, but..."

"No, Bob." Gabriel hadn't raised his voice but he had toughened up the consonants, stretched the words and was cutting through Bob's attempt at bonhomie. "You're not listening, Bob. I am REQUIRED to NOT reimburse you. It's out of my hands."

"I see what you're doing," said Bob. "But it's my money and I'll have it back now."

"Actually, no it isn't and I don't think I can return it."

"Are you having fun here, Gabriel? Are you enjoying trying to make me squirm? I'm not squirming, Gabriel. Do you think this is really going to end with you waltzing off to your own Caribbean island? It isn't, Gabriel. Really, it isn't. So have a good think, Gabriel, before you make your next little play."

"Bob, this is absolutely not about making you squirm. This is about me trying to abide by the contract that your company produced. I didn't even try to amend it! If only I'd known. Hang on, maybe I could... No, false alarm."

"What's the false alarm?"

"Well, apparently I have to refund any payment made for books which have been returned by the customer. But I'm guessing you haven't had any returns?"

It was at this point that they had an unfortunate

discussion about killing and Gabriel explained about the Post Office Regulation Elastic Band that was holding a lapel microphone against the earpiece of his phone and about the software on his computer that was displaying a bibbly-bobbly sharply-pointed green sound wave as it recorded and stored their conversation.

Bob Tucker founded Bob's Book Emporium in 1985 on Duke Street, just around the corner from where the Frenchgate Shopping Centre squats in the heart of Doncaster. He took over Duke Street Books and spread the Word Of Bob by edict to the staff, by posters and pennants throughout the shop, by advertising in the city and by word-of-mouth of satisfied customers. It was all about the range, the keen pricing, the no-nonsense customer service. Any book, quickly, and at the best possible price.

Mail-order led to call-centre-hothouse telephone ordering. Bob went global and the shop became Bob's Global Book Emporium. BGBE to its fans. BGreedyE to its unimaginative detractors, the envious, the chisellers, the ones who *should have done it themselves* if they were so clever. This was the third phase, or Day Three according to the Word Of Bob.

And, naturally, the shop closed in 1995 as Bob went virtual and lower-case. bgbe.com destroyed the competition the same way that Frenchgate had killed the high street three decades earlier.

And finally, Bob went both virtual and electronic

and the irritation of stock and packaging and couriers and customs declarations disappeared. Bob's Global E-Book Emporium or, more fashionably, bgebe.com was born.

A British success story. A global corporation with a string of letters but, unlike so many others, everyone knew what the first letter stood for, even if they lost track of the order of the other words. It was Bob's company, with his name above the virtual door, with his virtual face beaming from the virtual register.

"You've had a twenty-eight year run," said Gabriel.

"You've done your homework," said Bob.

"It's all over your website," said Gabriel. "I love your company. Every book I buy comes from you. I want to help. I'm sure we can compromise."

"You're not getting your name on the company," said Bob.

There was a large and official-looking group bustling along the corridor, sending people on their way, or out through side doors. Bob was going to be in the way.

"I don't want my name on the company," said Gabriel. It was his turn to laugh. "Hey Bob, apparently one of the minor royals is coming to your event."

"I'm sorry, sir, you're going to have to clear this corridor. Please return to your seat," said the man with the high-visibility jacket and the ear-piece.

"Do you mind?" said Bob. He clapped his hand over the phone, always favouring the old-school manual mute over some new-fangled button-pecking method. "I'm on the phone. Your little group can walk around me. I'm not in your way and this call is *far* more important than you could possibly realise."

Bob had a point. He was working to ensure the continued survival of a major UK-based global corporation which was in severe peril. At stake were jobs across the world, tax revenue and even the value of the stock options belonging to the newly unemployed Phil Leonard. You'd need extreme tunnel vision to automatically assume that Bob's conversation was less important than completely clearing the primary route of a slightly royal person. Other than journalists, fervent flag-wavers and her own staff, few people would even be able to pick her out of a loosely selected line-up.

Security personnel, however, pride themselves on extreme tunnel vision in the protection of their clients. And so it was that Bob's conversation with Gabriel was placed on hiatus when Bob found himself lying on the concrete floor with his arms twisted behind his back.

Afterwards, Bob wondered whether he should simply have used the old dependable "don't you know who I am?" line so beloved of minor celebrities in Tight Spots.

The charges against Bob were dropped like a

proverbial hot, and probably also rancid, potato. And Bob came to an understanding with Gabriel. The money was returned. bgebe.com didn't even go into overdraft at the bank.

But the money was only a loan from Gabriel Denton, formerly copywriter and social media facilitator, still aspirational author with unrealistic expectations. A repayment schedule for the loan was drawn up, perused by clever lawyers and agile accountants and declared fair and legal.

Having simple tastes, Gabriel divides his time between modest homes in Brittany and Umbria. He advertises his books in prime-time on commercial television but sells very few copies since good reviews from reputable journals are so hard to buy. He seeks out new authors and supports them in their early lean years. He works on his French and Italian.

And he looks after his health. Bob makes sure that Gabriel sees the best doctors for annual check-ups, and for the slightest of ailments.

Bob's chipping away at the debt. Gabriel's giving the outstanding balance back in his will. And the inheritance tax would knock down the company if it comes due any time this half-century.

So nobody died. Everything turned out okay.

Even Phil Leonard had a Happy Ending – he found another Louise to work for and they married two years later. He cashed in his stock options to buy a little house in the countryside. His little start-up web retailer launches later this year. Maybe, now, he knows more about how to do it than Bob.

Author's Note

This is a FICTITIOUS piece of whimsy. It is NOT based on anything real and is certainly NOT a thinly-veiled criticism of any retailer. This story came from my imagination. In the real world, I have only had positive interactions with retailers (both as a buyer and seller) and would not dream of criticising any of them.

And the David vs Goliath story is WELL out of copyright.

Ina and Kosta

Kosta first met Ina when he fell through the ceiling and landed gracefully and, some would say, stylishly, next to her on the sofa. The disadvantage of apartment-living immediately became clear. In a house, you'd always expect to know the person in the room above.

She put down her book and turned to look at him.

"Hello," he said. "I'm Konstantin. Call me Kosta." He offered his hand for shaking.

Whatever she might have said in reply was lost because a little of the ceiling chose that moment to wrench itself free and flutter down over them, as a magical white plasterboard snowstorm.

Kosta wasn't going to let an opportunity like this go to waste. "What are you reading?" he asked.

Later that day, as they sat in a local café and debated whether an insurance claim, a woodworm exterminator or a spiral staircase was called for, Kosta's phone rang. Many serious, furrow-browed mm-hmms and oh-yeses and even an occasional you-betcha later, he stood. His coffee was only three-quarters drained.

"I must go," he said. "I'd rather stay. But..."

He gestured towards the door. He overacted a sad face. He left. No floor-decision had been made.

Ina next met Kosta three weeks later. She had just parked her car. He was getting out of a taxi, smartly dressed, incongruously casual shoulder-slung messenger-bag swaying slightly. He paid the driver and turned.

"I finished your coffee," she said. She laughed, put her hand to her mouth, nearly resisted her eyes following his bag to and fro, to and fro. "Sorry, was that a strange thing to say?"

"Not at all," he said. "It would have been a shame to waste it. Sorry I had to go but..." He pointed vaguely at the departing taxi, then at his bag. "Shall we go in? We do live here, after all."

"My place is probably safer," she said. "There's a hole in your bathroom floor."

"Have you not had it fixed yet?" he asked. They were walking up the stairs. She turned to stare at him. When he knew her better, he would be able to safely identify it as mock outrage. But not today. "I'm sorry. I would have helped but I had to..."

She unlocked her door. "They needed access," she said. "I didn't know who to ask for a spare key. It didn't seem fair to have your door kicked in. What is even more interesting is *why* you fell through the floor."

She paused. He waited. He mouthed the word 'and?'. She smiled.

"There was the cheap vinyl sheet. And the cheap

ceiling board. But nothing in between," she said.

"Nothing in between?" he said.

"Nothing in between," she said. "The vinyl was very well attached at the edges of the room. But someone had walked across it in stilettos. And put in a line of perforations. A bit like an 'open here' on a chocolate box."

"I always thought it was quite..." he paused, searching for the next word. His bag still swayed slightly on his shoulder. On the fourth sway he continued. "Spongy," he said.

"Quite appropriate for a bathroom," she said.

"Yes," he said.

"Friend of yours?" she asked.

"Who?" he said.

"The stiletto wearer," she said.

"Probably Hana," he said.

Ina raised an eyebrow. Kosta paused to admire the asymmetry.

Then he said, "My friend's daughter. She was staying in my flat on and off last month. I wasn't there, seemed a shame to force her to pay for a hotel."

He looked up at the grey tape stretched across the hole.

"It's not pretty," she said, as the kettle juddered and whooshed in the kitchen, "but it's surprising how little you notice it after a day or two."

The kettle clicked, the roar subsided, Kosta turned his head slightly to one side and held his hand up, palm outwards, the internationally recognised appeal for stillness and hush. Ina almost said, "what?" or "why?" or some other word to convey her confusion at the sudden urgency of his need not just to listen but to *listen*.

But her lips froze at the beginning of the 'w' and there it was again, an illusion of outrage when all she was doing was following a reasonable instruction.

And, with a shrug, a mouthed apology which she interpreted more from expression than lip-reading, he was at the door and then he was gone.

Just after he had left, she heard it: the slightest creak, as though the ache of standing still and ready and alert had sought relief through a foot adjustment on a previously unremarked loose floorboard. Or perhaps it was just the building doing what buildings do as temperature and humidity and air pressure rise and fall.

She pushed the door firmly closed and heard the click of the lock and turned the key just to be certain. And she stood a while longer and listened – really listened carefully, the sort of listening that can only be done once the hair has been strictly pushed behind the ear and once the breathing has settled. But she heard nothing more.

And so Ina began to pull all the usual things from her handbag. Her phone went on the little table in the hall and her book went by her bed and then she remembered that the kettle had boiled and she walked, slowly and ever so slightly twirling, into the kitchen when all of a sudden she heard plenty.

At first it was as though the kettle was boiling again – but this time boiling like it meant it, with anger and fury and rage and roaring – until she realised that, of course, it wasn't the kettle at all. It was the hot air balloon just over her building with its basket right by her kitchen window with Kosta standing in it shouting to be heard over the noise.

She opened the window. "I can't hear you," she shouted.

"Get in," he shouted. "Don't go back for anything, just get in."

And she looked at him and, much to her surprise, she found herself clambering over the sink and draining board and squeezing through the window and taking his hand and skittering her feet over the sill and taking his other hand and jumping. As she jumped she heard a sound behind her – a sound she would not have been able to identify only a few weeks earlier but which she could now state with confidence was the sound of someone falling through her ceiling.

But the sounds and the ceiling and the kitchen were behind and below her as they rose higher and higher. Maybe she saw a face at her window. Maybe there were two faces. But they were receding, whereas she was ascending with a man she hardly knew. Oh, and with a young woman operating the burner. She looked over and smiled and once they had reached a good height (Ina was terrible at estimating distances but this was more than plenty double-decker buses high), the young woman shut off the burner and, in the calm, with only the rush of the wind and the occasional whinge of a seagull to trouble them, she said, "Hello, I'm Hana."

"Ah," said Ina. "Of course you are."

"I'm sorry if I startled you," said Kosta.

"Startled?" said Ina. "It was a little more than that."

"...but I thought escaping through the window would be less surprising than having Justin and Juergen dropping onto your sofa," said Kosta.

"And who are they?" said Ina. "I'm guessing not a comedy duo."

"Definitely not a comedy duo," said Hana. She looked over Ina's shoulder. "And their jokes are terrible too," she continued, firing up the burner. Even over the roar, Ina could hear the throbbing rumble of the helicopter. She looked around.

"Please tell me that's not..." she said.

"Okay, it's not," said Kosta.

"It's not what?" asked Ina.

"I don't know," said Kosta. "You just asked me to tell you that it wasn't, so I did. I'm obliging like that. But I suggest we do something about those two."

The helicopter was too close and the basket was swaying, buffeted violently by the down-draught.

And yet, still Justin tried to fly even closer so that Juergen could open the slide-back door in order to... In order to do what? Was he going to grab the basket, the ropes, Kosta, Hana, Ina? Who knew? He never had the chance because the rotors caught against the brightly coloured balloon, its rainbow stripes and curves bucked and split, sending the helicopter twisting away in a surprising spiral and sending the balloon downwards at a jaunty angle.

Over the roar of the wind, Hana shouted, "You okay?"

And Kosta and Ina answered together. Ina said, "Are you crazy?" and Kosta said, "Sure, I got this."

So Hana threw herself over the side of the basket and her parachute whoomped out behind her. Kosta, on the other hand, took a craft knife from his messenger-bag.

"Please stand as close to me as you possibly can," he said.

She moved closer, pressed herself tightly against him.

"Thank you," he said. Tying himself to her by wrapping two of the balloon's ropes three times around their upper-arms, he reached down and cut the ropes free from the basket. Their feet dangling freely, he pulled the ropes fiercely down towards him until what remained of the balloon was around them. He then cut a canopy shape and, with the last cutting flourish, it opened above them.

He tweaked and twitched at the ropes then

looked at Ina. "I'm sorry. I'm having all the fun. Would you like to take over with the steering?" he asked.

"Sure," she said. "This one seems a bit easier to steer than the last one I used."

"Good," he said. "I don't see why I should do all the work around here." He pulled his phone out of his pocket. "Give me a nudge if you need me to do anything," he said, then started pecking his fingers against the glass screen. This was quite awkward because the ropes were holding them together, face close to face – except now there was also a phone inconveniently close to Ina's chin.

She looked down. The view over the city was quite beautiful, if one she was not accustomed to. The river snaked through, looking surprisingly clean from this height. The buses looked irrelevantly small, the cars laughable, the pedestrians impossible to care for. The domes and the cupolas, the spires and the steeples were glorious. But she didn't aim for any of them. Instead, she landed them, quite smoothly and politely, on a riverbus.

"Excellent," said Kosta, slipping his phone back into his pocket before cutting them free from their parachute and starting to roll the material carefully. He bowed slightly to the applause from the tourists. "But I wish you'd taken us around one more time. I was about to get a perfect score on that level of Furious Monkeys."

"You should have said," said Ina, collapsing onto

the nearest bench. "Just as you really should have told me to put on my shoes before climbing out the window."

"Here, take these," said Kosta, retrieving a pair of stylish yet practical black leather shoes from his bag. "And can I have your number? I thought we could maybe..."

"Go for a normal night out?" said Ina. "Sure. Call me. I'm in the book."

"I will do that," he said, smiling. "But there's one thing you need to know."

"Oh really?" she said. "Just one?"

"Yes, just one," he said. "You can't ask me to explain, er..." He gestured vaguely around as though searching for the perfect way to sum up the one thing she was not allowed to have explained.

"This?" she said.

"Yes, this," he said, smiling. "All *this*."

And so three weeks and four meetings passed without mention of the balloon, the helicopter, the parachute, the boat, the flight, the chase or the plummet but there was plenty to say about hopes and dreams and plans and childhoods and dessert preferences and whether men can ever wear white socks and why people work five days each week instead of the six suggested by the bible and where the most ticklish spot was located and what could be done when the sea levels rise and how it was too late for hats to make a comeback and which city they should visit if they were to travel together.

Finally, in the café, with the staff cleaning and clearing for the night, putting everything back the way their colleagues had found it eighteen hours earlier, Ina and Kosta sat on plastic chairs, either side of a plastic table, counter on one side, floor-to-ceiling window on the other, with Kosta stirring his spoon around and around his cardboard cup to try to coax every last sugar crystal to abandon its corporeal form and float off freely into the coffee.

Ina said, "I have a confession to make."

And Kosta said, "Oh really?"

And Ina said, "Yes. I took the floorboards out."

And Kosta said, "I know."

And they might have kissed if only the door had not suddenly opened because, once Justin was sitting next to Kosta and Juergen was sitting next to Ina, it would have seemed awkward.

"Hello," said Juergen, offering his hand to Ina. She looked at it, then she looked at him. She did not move to shake it. He allowed it to fall gracefully into his lap. "I'm Juergen. It's lovely to finally catch up with you."

"Kosta," said Ina. "Maybe you should have explained *this* before *this* came to see us."

"Don't think badly of us," said Justin. "I'm Justin, by the way," he said, smiling. Ina did not return the smile.

"So what happens now?" she asked Juergen, before throwing her gaze across the table to give Justin the chance to answer, if he so chose. She did not look at Kosta, who showed no signs of wanting to say anything to anyone.

Later that evening, Kosta told her that "you should always keep your eye on the person who's *not* doing the talking because he's probably the one plotting something. Really the two J's should have known that. But I'm quite happy they didn't."

And later that evening, Ina said, "So are they after something in that bag? You always seem to carry it."

And later that evening, Kosta said, "You agreed that you wouldn't ask me to explain, er... *this*." And he said it with an apologetic face and she nodded and they smiled.

But earlier that evening, while they were sitting in the café and Kosta wasn't answering and Juergen was being charming with, perhaps a slight sarcastic edge to his voice and Justin was sitting and nodding, Ina asked, "So will you two explain what is going on here."

Justin said, "You mean he hasn't told you?"

And Juergen said, "You know, Kosta, that surprises me even more than the hot air balloon."

But still Kosta *said* nothing. Instead, he used his arms. He left arm punched out the window while his right arm grabbed Ina's right wrist and, within a heartbeat, or perhaps the time it takes to turn a page of an encyclopedia, or maybe the reaction time of a bird of prey, the two of them were out on the pavement and running, just running. And Ina was glad that she was wearing the sensible shoes although, once they had reached the car and were driving away, quickly, but not dangerously, she realised that the others hadn't chased them. So she could have worn the heels after all.

They overtook a bus and parked near the next stop. "Come on," said Kosta. "Time to change vehicle."

The bus took them to the station. Kosta stepped down to the kerb and turned to offer his hand to Ina. She took it, even though she was already standing beside him.

"How gallant," she said.

"Let's just go round here for a moment," said Kosta. Still holding her hand, which he had somehow neglected to release, he lead her around the side of the station, past a row of pastel-coloured dustbins and into a short dead-end footpath which terminated at a locked metal gate. "And let's not think about what normally happens around here," he said.

"I would guess that normally rubbish gets thrown away here," she said. "What were you going to dispose of?"

Instead of answering, Kosta reached into his bag and extracted a small parcel, tightly bound in dry-cleaner's polythene. He gave it to Ina.

"What's this?" she asked.

"New clothes," he said. "Do you like the ones you're wearing?"

"I did when I bought them," she said.

"And now?" he asked.

"I won't miss them," she said.

"Excellent," he said. "Please get changed. Everything. I'll turn around."

And so Kosta turned around and Ina waited for a moment and looked at his back and then decided that she would stay facing him. She tore into the plastic.

"You have good taste," she said. "Is it my size?"

"Of course," he said.

"Are you getting changed too?" she asked.

"No," he said. "There's no tracker in my clothes."

She undressed carefully, not rushing but not dawdling. She laughed.

"What is it?" he asked.

"Lucky it's a warm night," she said.

"Are you done yet?" he asked.

She waited, just a breath or two. He did not turn. "Not yet," she said.

He listened to the sound of fabric over skin, elastics stretching and relaxing, zips sliding, buttons pushed through. Then she tapped him on the shoulder.

"Ready?" he asked.

"What do you think?" she said.

He turned. "You look good and I have great taste," he said.

"You meant to say that I look great even in these,

frankly, average clothes that you've given me," she said.

"You can have it that way if you'd rather," he said.

She smiled and slightly curtsied. "You'll have to let me dress you some time," she said.

"Are you flirting with me?" he said.

"Of course," she said. "When *haven't* we been flirting?"

"It's a good question," he said, "but I can't answer that right now." He wrapped her old clothes in the polythene, twisting it around and around into a tight bundle. "You didn't have anything in the pockets?" he asked.

She smiled. "There weren't any pockets," she said, holding up her handbag.

Five minutes later, clutching a new handbag which had come from Kosta's bag and which was only large enough for absolute essentials, Ina watched as Kosta dropped the polythene-wrapped clothing and handbag bundle over the side of a bridge onto a departing train. It nestled cosily into a recess in the train roof. Kosta nodded.

Inside the station, Kosta bought two first-class tickets to the capital city of the neighbouring country. Then he turned to look at Ina.

"Or you could make your way home if you'd rather," he said. "I suppose I could have offered you that choice a little sooner."

"But I don't have anything better to do," she said.

She smiled. She pushed her hair behind her ear. She fidgeted her right foot from side to side, twist and straighten. Then she said, "I suppose it's lucky that I brought this, just in case." She pulled her passport from her new handbag.

"It's not lucky at all," said Kosta. "If you weren't the sort of person to bring it, I don't think this, er, *adventure* would have gone the way that it has."

Later that evening, Ina said, "Those clothes were a perfect fit."

And Kosta said, "If you think something is going to *matter*, you make sure you do it properly."

"So I've seen," said Ina. "Good night."

"Good night," said Kosta. He was lying beneath her. She had asked for the upper bunk. With his bag against the wall and his arm around the strap, he lay on his back, eyes closed, listening to the clickerty-clack of the wheels, the occasional flexing of the springs above him, the infrequent buffeting from passing another train, or entering a tunnel, or leaving a tunnel or perhaps just from the wind whipping and whooping around them.

Ina lay facing the window, on her side, knees drawn up almost to a foetal position, watching the rushing glows of street-lights and station-lights and traffic lights blurring past until the soothing hum of the motion and the warmth of feeling safe lulled her to sleep.

When she awoke, the sun filled the compartment and Kosta was looking out of the window. There were trees and an embankment but no other clues.

"Where are we?" she asked.

"Good morning," he said, turning around. "Nearly there. Thanks for coming."

"Like I said," she said, "I didn't have anything better to do." She swung her legs over the side of the bed and smoothed her sleep-crumpled clothes. "But reassure me that we're going to leave the train through the door rather than the window."

Hand on chest and eyebrow raised in affront, Kosta said, "Well, clearly we will. Besides, train windows are laminated and toughened and I don't have a coffee spoon concealed in my palm today. And this glass isn't already cracked."

As they left the station, stepping out into the chaos and bustle and chatter and roar, they both spoke at the same time.

Kosta said, "Where would you..." but he stopped mid-sentence because Ina was saying, "Isn't that Justin on the other side of the road?" and because she was pointing and because she was right.

Some time later, Ina realised that pointing had been a very bad idea because it made them stand out in the crowd which led to Justin nudging Juergen who turned around, gave a small nod of recognition and the two of them began the not inconsiderable job of shouldering their way through the people and nearly stationary vehicles. Leading a pair of dogs did not make the task any easier.

Needless to say, Kosta and Ina were running, zigzagging along the pavement, turning right here, crossing a road there, before finding themselves at the entrance to a large park. With a judicious cry of 'this way!', Ina veered off to one side.

"We should rent these," she said, somewhat breathlessly.

"I'm not very good on those," said Kosta.

"Oh really?" said Ina, hands on hips, shoulders back. "Have I found something you can't do?"

"But I'm sure it'll be fine," said Kosta, reaching into his pocket and handing over the cash. He then parted with considerably more when the attendant pointed to the bottom of the tariff board.

"I'm not convinced you're going to get that deposit back," said Ina.

"Never mind," said Kosta. "It's still good value for a pair of roller-blades."

"Two pairs," said Ina.

"I'm *not* keeping these," said Kosta. He was some distance behind her. Perfect graceful balance was eluding him. Two men and two dogs were within sight behind them.

"Oh come on," said Ina, returning, twirling neatly and grabbing his arm. "Lean on me if you must."

And so off they skated across a beautiful park, flowers blooming around them, blossom sprinkling like ceiling plaster over their heads, the rich smell of freshly-cut grass enveloping them, the excited chatter and laughter of children all around. If they hadn't been trying to elude two men and their dogs, it could have been idyllic. At least the dogs were being kept on a lead.

If Kosta could have kept himself upright, unsupported, that would also have been a bonus. But he found he didn't mind keeping his arm around Ina, his hand occasionally tightly gripping her shoulder. She wasn't objecting, nor did she suggest at the time that he could probably skate just fine and was using this fake incompetence strategically.

But she did ask him later. "Was that just an excuse to put your arm around me?"

"By that time, did I need an excuse?" he asked.

Once they had reached the other side of the park and were passing through its ornate gates and twisting on their heels to wait for a gap in the traffic, Kosta was slightly less likely to fall over. But as they crossed the road and turned left, he realised that the gradient was increasing. There was no avoiding it. He was hurtling, more or less out of control, down a hill.

"Do you..." shouted Ina.

"I can't..." shouted Kosta.

Her skating was aggressive and relentless and pounding as she thumped and pushed and slid along the pavement but his brute flailing and extra momentum were winning out. The architecture around them was striking and impressive, baroque, then modernist, then concrete, then steel-and-glass. Marble and stone were of less interest than the approaching intersection and, somewhat implausibly, two men standing behind a van who suddenly finished wrestling with their delivery and turned a large sheet of glass across Kosta's path.

"No!" he shouted. "I can't stop."

The men holding the glass froze in disbelief at the sight of a roller-blading novice hurtling towards them.

Kosta managed to turn to the left as they tried to manhandle the glass the same way. He turned to the right as they moved that way too. He waved his arms in a frenzied windmill of frustration but still they dodged and thrusted this way and that.

He gave up the amateur semaphore in favour of good old-fashioned shouting.

"Will you *please* stand still and let me try to get round you?" he bellowed.

Clearly they didn't quite understand because the left-right dodging continued for a few more tantalising seconds before they suddenly realised the simple solution and turned the glass around. Side on, it made a far smaller target and one that Kosta had no trouble not hitting.

Unfortunately, it just meant that he collided with the side of a bus instead which had just turned into the road which Kosta should have crossed in a more controlled manner. He slumped to the ground, Ina whisked up alongside him and, together, they climbed onto the bus. The doors closed. A long way behind them, at the top of the hill, they caught a brief glimpse of two men running, then walking, then stopping, dogs running around their ankles.

Also unfortunately, roller-blades were not the best footwear for Kosta while standing in a crowded moving bus.

And later, in a comfortable yet surprisingly reasonable city-centre hotel, she said, "Can you explain the dogs at least?"

And Kosta, lying on his back, hand between head and pillow, elbow pointing straight into the bathroom, said, "They're beagles."

"That wasn't the explanation I was hoping for," said Ina. She lay beside him, her head by his feet, her feet by his head.

"Great at picking up a scent," said Kosta. "That could be how they followed us at the station – ignored the tracker and used the dogs to pick out the platform. Or..."

"Yes?" asked Ina, lifting her head slightly to see over his feet, to see if his expression was worth reading.

"Or there never was a tracker on you so they were always planning on using the dogs," he said. He smiled. It *could* have been an apologetic smile.

"So I got changed and threw away some of my favourite clothes for nothing?" she asked.

"You said you wouldn't miss them," he said, lifting his head too, staring her in the face, trying to work out whether she was serious.

"I was being *polite*," she said, flopping her head

back down either in annoyance or because her neck was getting achey.

"And don't forget about the guy who watched it all on CCTV," said Kosta.

"I'm going to assume that's a joke," said Ina.

He nudged her shoulder with his foot. "Cheer up," he said. "I've got a couple of things to tell you."

She sat up. "This sounds like it calls for my full attention," she said, straightening her back and fixing a stare firmly onto his face.

"Well," he said, "technically it's one thing to tell you and one thing to ask you."

And in that hotel, on that night, Kosta told Ina everything that he hadn't yet told her and then he asked her the one thing he hadn't yet asked her. And Ina said yes and a few (but not too many) months later, in a church by the sea, they were married.

Justin and Juergen were there, although the beagles had been left back at home. Hana sat in the same row.

And later, much later, when there were speeches and eating and dancing and more speeches, Kosta told the guests how they had met while working for the same company (even on the same floor) and how it was love at first sight. The last part was true. And there *was* a floor involved in the process.

Then Ina stood up and said that Kosta had told them a pile of lies and that they had actually met when Kosta fell through her ceiling, which got a laugh although she knew that wasn't the whole truth either. She had watched him from her window for weeks before acquiring the tools, removing a few planks, positioning her sofa and waiting.

And he had arranged a little adventure to get to know her better before he really even knew her at all. He'd only seen her staring absent-mindedly (or so he thought) out of her window. Of course, once he'd landed on her sofa, he knew she was the right person for him.

But clearly there was no point in telling anyone the whole truth because no one would ever believe it.

Instead, the 'meeting at work' story was safe, dull and reassuring – and, with a light sprinkling of 'love at first sight', it was just right for general consumption, perfectly easy to spin into a detailed and humorous anecdote. But what did it matter what other people thought, or knew, or thought they knew? As long as Ina and Kosta knew that everything would turn out just fine.

Slightly Disappointed

Be reasonable, be specific and be nice. Not the best slogan that he had ever heard but shorter than some and clearer than most. How could he spread the word?

He settles on the classified advertisements in the local paper. So reasonable for seven specific words and a phone number that he pays extra for bold printing and a nice little box around it. Five people phone. One makes a rude noise. One tries to sell him insurance. Three arrive for the inaugural meeting. He letters them for convenience and anonymity. If they return he'll find out their names. For now, they are B, C and D. He, of course, is A. A for Adam, the first man. He smiles at the prescience of his parents.

8pm on a Wednesday. They are sitting around his glass coffee table, drinking his tea, ignoring his biscuits, wondering who is going to speak first. Eye contact is fleeting and uncertain.

"So what's this all about?" asks B. Adam knows he is a terrible judge of age. She could be anywhere from mid-thirties to early-fifties. Her hair is plaited but not quite straight. It pulls to the right, as though attracted to the handbag, wedged tightly under the elbow, its strap still over the shoulder. Her posture appears spirit-level vertical.

"Nice cup of tea," says C, smiling. Even Adam can tell that he is over fifty, maybe as much as seventy. His close-cropped hair has receded well over the crown of his head. The hounds-tooth jacket needs replacing.

"How reasonable, specific and nice of you," says D, smiling then looking down to his slightly discoloured trainers. "Sorry, that came out sounding all sarcastic. It didn't sound like that in my head." He may not be aware that the tangled, matted hair on the top of his head only partially hides the emerging bald patch. The heavy-knit sweater nearly matches the corduroy trousers.

"I'm not going to be mysterious," says Adam, half-heartedly reaching his hands out in a welcoming gesture before quickly letting them drop into his lap. "But I'd love to know what you were expecting before I tell you."

"Some sort of volunteer, charity thing?" says C.

"Campaigning group," says B. "And I love the way that 'reasonable, specific and nice' doesn't rule out passive-aggressive." She does the bunny-ear fingers to hang the quotation marks in the air.

"I'll tell you later," says D, blushing slightly and leaning his cheek on his palm, elbow on his leg which, in turn, is crossed over the other leg as though he could cover his embarrassment using contortion.

"No need unless you want to," says Adam. He clears his throat, smiles, looks down into his lap, looks up again. "Sorry, never done anything like this before. Haven't heard much preaching outside the usual places so haven't really got any template to follow."

"Preaching?" asks B.

"Non-denominational," says Adam quickly. "I don't judge, they're all good as far as I'm concerned."

"Well how very generous of you," says B. "And I'm not sorry if that sounded sarcastic."

"Please be nice," says D, still staring at his shoes.

"No, that's fair enough," says Adam, still smiling. "But please let me get a bit further before you shoot me down." He's not only looking at B, he's looking around the room, equal time on each face and some time not looking at anyone in particular. "At least let me get a bit more of the target up first."

C chuckles. B nods but says nothing. D waits.

"I'd love to say that it doesn't matter if you have faith or not but I don't think I can," says Adam, slowly and carefully, as though picking his words precisely. The rest comes out quickly. "I think they're all true and that people have been given the one they should follow but that sometimes they change and that's okay too. It's all directed at the same place."

"So you're a bit evangelical but not for any faith in particular?" asks B.

"Yes," says Adam.

"Carry on," says B.

"Are you chairing this meeting?" asks C, chuckling again. Something in his tone of voice lets him get away with this question. Adam wishes he knew how to do it. D might have gulped but it might have been a withheld cough.

"Not yet," says B, smiling. "Carry on." She relaxes a little, her back loosens, she nearly reclines into her chair but corrects for it. And the thin, tight smile does not last long.

"How about Norse?" asks D.

No one groans but an uncomfortable silence follows. D looks up, eyes widening imploringly as the seconds tick by, as his question hangs in the air.

"The language or the gods?" asks C, getting away with it again.

"I think they were valid too," says Adam. "But that's not the main point I'm trying to make here."

D nods but does not risk another comment.

"I want to talk about letters of complaint," says Adam. "I've written enough of them. Did you all know that the successful letter of complaint is all about disappointment? It's not about anger. It's about inconvenience, and doesn't pretend it's about catastrophe. It asks for something reasonable, doesn't just try to get as much money as it can."

This comes out easily, it has been well rehearsed

in Adam's head over many years.

C breathes in as though about to speak but then doesn't.

"So it is campaigning," says B, sitting up straighter, showing that it was possible.

"And I also want to talk about prayer," says Adam.

B slumps into her seat and, putting her hand to her face, starts massaging the inside corners of her eyes between thumb and forefinger. C leans forward slightly. D has frozen since his Norse faux-pas and is still staring intently.

"People ask for too much and they ask the wrong way. That's why prayer doesn't work," says Adam, keen to get to the point, keen to face the ridicule if it is coming.

Adam pauses, allows interruptions. None come.

He tells them about his moment of realisation. He had written a simple letter of complaint.

"And as I posted the letter, literally as it slid into the mouth of the postbox, it came to me," says Adam, wide eyed, hands twitching to gesticulate but held back by embarrassment. "Here I was, asking the car park operators for a refund. They'd charged me twice."

"You too?" asks C. "I wonder whether they do it on purpose. I call it strategic incompetence."

"How cynical of you," says B. "Normally I'm the only person in the room to have those sorts of thoughts."

"But," continues Adam, nodding at, but waving away, their comments, "I didn't write my letter congratulating the car park operator on the glory and wonder of their tarmac and line painting and their generously low pricing and the beauty of their advertising – and then slip in a quick sentence about being overcharged at the end. Of course I didn't! That wouldn't have worked. At best they'd have thought I was being sarcastic."

"Nope," says C. "They would have gone for oddball or unhinged straight away."

"Exactly," says Adam. "So it's hardly surprising prayers go unanswered. They're so crushingly dull! Paragraph after paragraph of creeping and crawling, the same every day, and then some desperate pleading at the end. As a spoken letter of complaint it fails in every way. This was the Realisation." He stresses the word. He wants them to know he's given it a capital letter.

But still the ridicule doesn't come. "People need to be, well, reasonable, specific and nice."

And he tells them about the Proof.

Eleven years earlier he had been out, walking. It didn't matter where he was going or from where he had come. He had no coat. He came out of a shop or a subway or a block of flats and the rain was relentless. There had been no sign it was coming. He had brought no coat, he tells them again in case they missed it first time around. He was not carrying an umbrella. He stayed under the porch or the awning or the eaves for as long as they lasted and, without breaking stride, he stepped out for his soaking, thinking that it would be lovely to stay dry. Some would call it a little prayer. And he stayed dry. He was following one stride behind the cloud edge. The rain had to stop somewhere – and it stopped right there because he'd politely asked it to. This was the Proof.

He hadn't really thought of it as a Proof until he had had the Realisation. Only two weeks earlier it had merely been a dinner-party anecdote.

And he tells them that big requests are never going to fly. You wouldn't try to return a thirty-year-old kettle that had been dropped and had smashed so why would you pray for the continued life of a sick hundred-and-three year-old? And he says that you wouldn't ask to be able to fly because, well, because you already can if you get into an aeroplane and that the other kind just isn't a reasonable thing to ask for.

He hadn't properly planned and formatted and structured what he was going to say and it doesn't have a proper beginning, middle and end and he had interruptions at the start and it all gets a bit raggedy and then sort of just stops.

But despite all that, even B seems won over. She's gone a bit misty-eyed. D is nodding and C is saying something about him really having something there.

"Small things," says C. "That's where the future

is."

"I don't know what you mean," says D to C. "But," he continues, "I like what you said, Adam. You've got a cold coming, haven't you?"

And until D had pointed it out, Adam hadn't really noticed or thought about it but, yes, there was a little catch in his voice and an occasional sniff and a thickness in his vowels. Adam nods.

"Well, we know there's no cure for the common cold," says D. He tries a half-laugh, which doesn't quite come out right but C chuckles and that covers the gap. "But some colds come and go quickly. I'd like to pray for a quick coming and going for Adam's cold. And I'll be disappointed and saddened if that can't be arranged." He glances upwards. "Am I supposed to look up or down when I say this?" he asks Adam.

"I don't know. I can't see why it would matter," says Adam. "And thank you for the kind thought."

"I'd like to add an Amen to that little prayer," says C. "And I'd like to hope that little prayers to help others have more chance than just selfishly asking for stuff for yourself." He pauses. "But I don't mind if anyone wants to ask for a little something for me."

B looks at him, frowning slightly. "I'm sorry, are you joking? It's just that you normally chuckle when you're trying to be funny," she says. She fiddles with her hair but that plait is never going to be straight unless she takes it apart and reties it.

"I was joking," says C, "but I'd like to offer a little prayer that maybe you figure out what to do about what's bugging you. And you don't need to tell us anything about it and I'm not asking."

"Amen to that," says D, although he looks away when B turns to stare at him. "I mean, I'd hope that everyone could figure out what to do, I'm not trying to criticise or anything."

"Thank you," says B, smiling for only the second time. "I mean, this is the most English, middle-class cult anyone could ever dream up – but it's no less charming for that."

"*Is* this a cult?" asks D. He looks either confused or worried. "That couldn't be much more different from what I was expecting."

"Does this mean you're finally going to tell us what you were expecting?" asks C.

There is a pause while the others wait for a chuckle which, this time, doesn't come.

"Oh, all right," says D. "I thought it was going to be a dating service."

"A dating service?" asks Adam. His voice climbs the scale across the three words. "Really?" He pauses. "Yes, I can see that. Reasonable, specific and nice could be three words of advice for dating." He smiles, his voice has returned to its usual register. "I'm sorry for disappointing you."

"Oh, don't be sorry," says D. "This is..."

"Surprising?" says C.

"Stimulating?" says B.

"Startling?" says Adam.

"Nice," says D. "Sorry. Quite a dull word. But it seems to fit."

"No need to apologise for calling something nice," says C. He chuckles. "Oh, please excuse me. I've had a bit of a cold myself. Left me with a slight cough, like my words keep tickling my throat on the way up and out."

"That's not a chuckle?" asks B, quickly and urgently.

"No, ma'am," says C.

"Then I apologise for what I said earlier," says B.

"What did you say earlier?" asks C. He appears to have no idea, his face has an open expression, his eyes are slightly widened with interest. D leans forward a little in anticipation of the great melting of B.

"I made a snide comment about you chuckling when you thought you were being funny. I apologise. It was unnecessary, it was rude and, if you have a sore throat, it was cruel as well," says B. A desperate earnestness was darting about her face while she was speaking, raising eyebrows, sucking in lips, flaring nostrils.

"Come come," says C. "It could hardly be called cruel. But I accept your apology even while I feel you have less to apologise for than you think."

"Thank you," says B. She rubs her eye, possibly smoothing a little moisture through the eyeliner.

"So what happens next?" asks C. He is looking

directly at Adam. It is a hard and concentrating look, not unkind but not relaxed. The answer had better be good.

"Well, er," says Adam, startled to realise that he hadn't predicted this entirely obvious question. "I think we need to think about, er..."

"If you don't mind my interrupting," says B, finding a warm smile to lubricate the words, "I think you're not sure and I don't think there's any shame in that. You have had a Realisation and you've shared it with us and, even if we don't all agree with every part of it, there clearly is a lot of good in it."

"Some of us might agree with every part of it," says C. He chuckles. "Excuse me."

"And I'm not saying we don't or that we shouldn't," says B. The smile has not been dented. "I'm just saying that much of it works either way. And I think we should keep up the praying but I think we need to add something else."

"Uh oh," says D. He tries to say it under his breath but it has clearly been heard. Adam stiffens his shoulders, B's eyebrows twitch and C chuckles, or perhaps he coughs. But no one takes offence and no one criticises. Perhaps D prayed that they wouldn't.

"We need to offer something back," says B. "If we're going to ask for little things for ourselves and for people that we know..."

"And sometimes for people that we don't know," says C.

"Yes," says B, "clearly." She clears her throat. "Then we need to find little good deeds we can do too."

"As an exchange?" asks D.

"Not really," says B. "More on an as and when basis. Goodness me, that's a tongue-twister."

She laughs. It turns out that this is the first genuine laugh of the evening and it has come from B. Perhaps, in some way, C's prayer, backed by D, has been answered.

"If all cults were like this, maybe people wouldn't be scared of them," says Adam, laughing. "I'm so relieved that you all turned out to be nice people and I really think this might lead somewhere. So this cult just does small random good deeds whenever it can and makes little prayers for reasonable, specific, nice things."

"How about getting more members? Isn't that the other thing cults do?" asks D. He looks hopeful – maybe his hope of finding a date was only knocked out temporarily, rather than flattened.

"I see no harm in it," says Adam. "But we're never going to do the bad thing that cults do. No one ever pays anyone and we don't ever disapprove of each other's families or friends."

"I think I'm immune to that anyway," says D. A brief silence follows. "Sorry, was that too pathetic to be funny?"

"It's just inaccurate," says C. "There are three of us in this room. And I think there are more to come."

"I've got some ideas about improving your newspaper ad," says B.

"You're just the sort of people I was praying for," says Adam.

"We should have a website," says D. "I can look after that. But we should have a name. Reasonable, specific and nice. RSAN, RSN, ar-san, sounds too much like arson."

"It needs to be intriguing and a little cool. But not too cool," says B. "We don't want to attract the wrong sort of person."

"There is no wrong sort of person," says Adam.

"Oh but there is," says C. "Maybe we can offer remedial work on damaged psyches when we're up and running but not now. Not while we're just getting started."

"Did you really just say 'damaged psyches'?" asks Adam.

"Yes," says C. "No point beating about the bush. The sort of person who's looking for a real hard-core culty cult. We can't handle their sort yet so best if we don't attract them."

"We turn no one away," says Adam, as firmly as he's said anything this afternoon. But that wasn't quite the question and he doesn't say anything more.

"I'd like to pray for a little bit of guidance on the name," says B. "I don't mind which one of us gets the idea. And I won't take any credit by saying it's because of this little prayer. But it would be great if someone could just get a good idea so we could move on."

"Amen," says C.

"Amen indeed," says Adam.

"Slightly disappointed," says D.

"Pardon?" says Adam.

"We're Slightly Disappointed. Are you slightly disappointed? There is a way through it. Join us," says D.

"I *do* like that," says B, not only smiling but beaming. C catches her eye and smiles too. When he smiles the years fall away and perhaps he could be early-fifties. Maybe late-forties even.

"That seems to be unanimous," says Adam. "Thank you. Do we have enough to work with?"

B and D nod. A clear strong "yes" comes from C.

"Same time next week then," says Adam. "In this room. Assuming you don't mind me running the meetings."

"Mind you running the meetings?" says C. "This is your cult, man. You're our leader. And while we like where you're leading us, we follow. Isn't that right?"

"Absolutely," says B.

"Certainly," says D. "Although when we disagree, we cook you and eat you."

Everyone laughs, including B. A warm feeling fills the room.

B gets up to leave. C helps her on with her jacket

and asks whether she has had dinner. She hasn't. He asks her if she'd like to try a restaurant a short walk away. He has heard good things about it. She says she would be delighted. They leave, C almost putting his arm around her shoulder while opening the door for her but allowing it to brush her coat as she passes without further incident.

Adam looks at D.

"I'm Dominic," says D. "We'll have to find out who they are next week. Did they arrive together or did something happen here tonight?"

"Clearly two people's prayers might have been answered," says Adam. "But it appears that the two of us end the evening slightly disappointed."

Kettle's On

The roar and whoosh of the kettle hides the chatter from outside. She boils it repeatedly while warming her hands on the coffee mug. She keeps away from the window.

The vans, the cars, the huddle, sometimes on the pavement, sometimes in the garden, occasionally opening the letter box – always for posting something through, never for a look, officer. The notes, the scrawls, the requests, the abuse – she thought it would die away, she thought it would recede, she thought something more important would be happening somewhere that might take some of them away at least for some of the time. It hasn't happened yet.

The chatter runs up a crescendo, the next programme contains stroboscopic flashes, the lightning bolts frame the curtains in clinical white and then he is at the door and his key is in the lock and he is inside.

The door closes, she moves to the hallway. She hears him turn and open the curtain, the ugly curtain which she hates, which has taken three feet off her hall, which hangs black and forbidding but opaque and comforting. The black curtain guards her privacy. It does the job that the law cannot and will not do.

She moves towards him, her footfall faltering as she gets nearer, she stops well outside his personal space. He makes no move to raise his arms to shake hands, pat on the shoulder, brief hug or shoulder-shuddering cuddle. He barely smiles, a tiny twitch at the edge of the mouth, a slight rise of eyebrow, a barely perceptible nod of the head.

"Well?" he says.

"That's not much of a greeting," she says. She smiles. "Yes, I'm getting by, thank you."

"And is there any *news*?" He shrugs his overcoat from his shoulders and adds it to the wide collection of never-worn coats which hang on the once-fashionable line of bright hooks.

"Another atrocity in the Middle East," she says.

"About *you*," he says, even the thin smile having faded, his voice squeezing out through his teeth, becoming more nasal in its disapproval.

"Ah!" she says and she laughs but it comes out a little too loudly and sounding a little too forced and she stops laughing a little too quickly. "I'm doing very well. I've discovered all sorts of things this morning. It's not just good for food shopping, you know. This internet – I can buy almost anything."

"Really? Gone on a shopping frenzy, have you?" He looks at her mug, its steam wisps still hopping over the rim. "Got any decent coffee or still drinking that value muck?"

He walks into the kitchen, flicks on the kettle, opens the cupboard and selects a mug, one from the second row, decorated with the silhouette of a stately home – the mug and the building both relics from a happier past. He stands and stares at the various boxes of fruit-infested teas, weighing them up against the plainly packaged supermarket own-brand coffee. He chooses a teabag from one of the brighter boxes. The leaves are enclosed in a silken purse, its twisted thread stapled to an overly cheerful tag.

The kettle boils very quickly.

"It was already hot, wasn't it?" he asks.

She nods.

"Your electricity bill's going to go through the roof," he says.

"But I can lower it, can't I?" she says, gazing at him but not getting an expression of approval in return. "I can change supplier, apparently. I'm not sure how it can be worth getting all the cables taken out and being attached to another company's electricity. But I read that I can save hundreds of pounds every year."

"You don't need to change the cables," he says. "You just change the bills."

"What sense does that make?" she asks.

"What do you mean?" he asks.

"I buy electricity from someone else but it still comes down the same cable from the same place –

how can that make any sense? What's changed?"

"You get a different colour ink on your bill and a different bunch of charming but ultimately powerless employees will answer the phone whenever you call them to tell them they've overcharged you." He sighs. "Those are the main changes. It's just a game. There must have been games like this years ago. The games have just moved on a bit. And got faster-moving. And there are more of them."

He pours the water slowly over his teabag and wrinkles his nose as the pungent fruity aroma wafts.

"They're still just as noisy," he says, gesturing towards the window. "What time does it quieten down at night?"

"I don't know," she says. "I don't stay up and watch. They're out there when I go to bed and they're out there when I get up. I can only stay in here if I put the kettle on to drown them out. I tried the radio but it's so gloomy these days. Did they always have so much news? So little fun and piffle..."

"Yes," he says. "Let's go into the lounge."

It is dusty in the lounge, the occasional stray shafts of sunlight catch the specks and there are lines on tables where dinner trays have kept dust at bay, or where magazines have rested for a while before being moved, to be filed with their dust in dusty racks where they may ever so slowly curl in dusty corners.

Even the day after she left, when he had come in to look at the place, to work out what needed to be done, to secure and log and tidy and cover and wrap, the rooms were spotless. Even when she should have been packing and considering and relaxing (as best she could), she had remained loyal to her standards. He had sat in the armchair on that day, ignored the cold and the silence, and wondered at the power of distraction therapy, the ability to keep on with the usual routine and act as though, while the cleaning and the vacuuming and the polishing can continue, everything must be just fine, the outside world kept at bay just a little longer.

He had come in when he could and tidied sporadically and superficially – a gesture towards what she would have done if only she could have been there. Over the years he couldn't remember changing the vacuum cleaner bag.

There had been no burst pipes during the many winters. He had kept the house at a healthy, if not luxurious temperature. He had paid for proper appliance inspections from properly qualified engineers – the sort who might not wear a uniform with their name sewn into the breast pocket but for whom an annual inspection means a strip-down, clean and reassemble, rather than opening the cupboard to check it's still there.

"You don't have to come every day," she says.

"I know," he says. "But I will."

She looks at him but his expression is giving

nothing away. His mouth is flat, his brow is smooth, his breathing is regular, his blinking is occasional. His mug is steady as he brings it to his mouth for a small sip.

"Thank you," she says, "but you know I could..." She pauses, looks up at him, smiles and waits for an interruption. It doesn't come. "...manage," she says.

"Of course you could," he says. "I know you can manage because I'm not doing very much and you clearly *are* managing. But I'm here in case you need me."

"Thank you," she says.

"But why is it so dusty in here?" he asks. He looks her in the eye, studying her expression. He turns his head every so slightly to one side.

"What do you mean?" she says. She keeps her head still and level.

"You know what I mean," he says. "You're not cleaning."

"I suppose it's one of the things that has stopped being important to me," she says. She smiles. "It turned out that the habit *could* be broken. There weren't any dusters there. And I began to find the smell... comforting. Then I stopped noticing it."

"It's as easy as that?" he asks. There's nearly a smile, or maybe just a slight tic at the corner of his mouth.

"It is," she says. She clears her throat and says, "but you're welcome to pick up a duster any time you like. You know where they are, don't you?"

He grunts. It is, perhaps, an approving noise.

She nods and says, "I think I'll change the subject and ask you whether you like my new chair."

He looks around the room, exaggerating his gestures, peering into each corner. He would have seen a new chair when he came in. It is not a large room.

"Is it very small?" he asks.

"No, it's upstairs," she says. "New bedroom chair. Didn't you wander upstairs last time you were here? I assume you have a poke around, make sure I'm not keeping the electric heater too near the bath or stockpiling painkillers or anything like that."

"I do not *poke around*," he says. "And I didn't see your chair. And why didn't you ask me about it last time I was here?"

"Because I was still thinking it over," she says, trying a half-smile.

"What is there to think about?" he asks, frowning. It is the first clear expression she has noticed. The crack in his impassivity seems to goad her on.

"The men who brought it," she says, starting slowly. "I ordered it on the line. Or do I say 'on-line'? It's 'on-line', isn't it? I thought it looked wide and deep and comfy and it wasn't too expensive and I thought I could probably send it back if it felt too hard. I should have phoned to check that but I didn't." She is speaking quickly now. "The men arrived and the crowd parted to let them through with the big box. The big exciting box. And when they came in, they looked at me, you know, the way that people look at me now, that almost-recognition, except these two men had the clues, didn't they? They had seen the crowd outside and they had read my *name* on the delivery note. They put it together."

He is standing now and moving towards her. He crouches down by her and takes her hand between his.

"The older one was all right," she continues, giving him her hand without commenting, not slowing, not quite looking him in the eye, "but the younger one worked it out and was staring and even though the older one was very much business-like and 'where would you like it, love?' and 'shall we put the legs on it for you, love?' and 'don't worry, we'll take away the packaging, love', the younger one had this *look* on his face."

He gives her hand a squeeze but still says nothing, lets her continue with the story. She doesn't give him a chance to smile reassuringly because she is now even further from looking him in the eye. She is studying the far top corner of the room, where a cobweb hangs, raggedy and forlorn, its landlord absent.

"And finally he says, the younger one says, 'Are you?' and I say, 'Yes, of course I am,' and he says, 'So did you?' and the older one says, 'I don't think that's any of our business, Michael,' and the older one turns to me and says, 'We're done here' and they pick up all the packaging and they leave and I find a little piece of torn cardboard that's fallen from their grip and I just sit on the floor and hold it. I sit on the floor *next to* my lovely new chair. I haven't sat *in* it yet."

He's looking directly at her but she doesn't know because the cobweb still holds her attention and he says, "Well you know that's silly. Go and try it now."

But she says, "Would you go upstairs and tell me if I chose well, if it's as comfy as it looks, if it needs to go back. If it needs to go back, will you be here? Can you speak to them? Can I just sit in the lounge with my back to the door?"

"...and pretend that the monsters aren't there as long as you can't see them?" he asks.

"I know damn well that the monsters are there but that doesn't mean I have to look at them," she says, her gaze fixed hard on the slowly flapping web. As she stares, it comes loose and gradually, sailing on the radiators' convection currents, it flutters down and down until she loses it against the patterned wallpaper.

"My friend tried that," he says. "Elliot – remember him?" She nods. "His daughter wouldn't settle one night, wouldn't close her eyes, screamed if he left the room – he didn't know what spooked her."

"It comes and it passes," she says. "There's no

right way to handle it as long as it's done kindly."

"But there's a wrong way," he continues. "Elliot told her, and he told her kindly, that she should shut her eyes because the *monsters will only go for her if she looks at them*. And as the words came out, he knew it was wrong but he didn't know how to undo the damage."

There is a pause.

"Wow," she says. "That's not going to end well."

"It hasn't ended well yet," he says. "I'm sure that they'll laugh about it in ten or thirty years' time. But right now he's got a daughter waking several times every night and bawling with her eyes tight shut. The terror of what she can't see and the panic of what will happen if she looks."

"I wouldn't know what to suggest to him," she says, shaking her head.

"You could tell him why you won't try your new chair," he says. "And why you wouldn't look at the men if they have to come back to collect it. Isn't that you shutting your eyes so the monsters won't see you?"

She says nothing.

"Come on – we'll try it together," he says, "but first tell me the other bit."

This catches her attention. A little rapid blinking, perhaps to reabsorb the nearly-fallen tears, or perhaps because of a fleck of dust, and she looks at him. "What other bit?"

"Something happened afterwards, didn't it?" he

asks.

She nods. "I heard them. And it was the older one. I thought it would be the younger one. But it was the older one, the one who wasn't called Michael. And there he was, talking to *them* outside. Describing my new chair. Describing how I'm wearing my hair and how I'm dressed and what I sounded like and..."

He stands up and pulls her up with him. "Enough!" he says. "We must reclaim your chair for you! You need to sit in it, and drink some tea and curl up with your book and then I'll come back downstairs and see if there's anything important in the post. It's *your* chair and it's probably a *good* chair and whether you like it or not has nothing to do with what Michael's mate might have said about you. And you know all this already but those words had to be said out loud and I've said them now so let's get on with it."

She looks at him. "You never asked," she says.

They are standing quite close together. British personal space would demand another few inches. She has the armchair behind her. And he does not shuffle back.

"I never asked what?" he asks. "Come on, let's go upstairs."

"No," she says, and she says it calmly but firmly and it is a very different tone of voice and it surprises him into stepping back, just a little but enough for comfort, and enough for her to breathe more easily. "You never asked."

He nods. "That's right," he says. "But what of it?" he says. "You want to talk about this *now*?" he says. "With *them* outside," he says.

"Yes."

"But *I* don't." He smiles as he says this; it is a smile with his lips but not with his eyes and she finally sees the demonstration of that hoary old truism. "Come on – I want to see your new chair."

He lets go of her hands, but gently – a releasing, not a discarding – and makes his way towards the stairs but she does not follow. She opens her mouth, the words almost escaping, then closes it and starts again.

"Now look what you've done," she says. "You nearly made me say a rude word. Damn the chair! This is not about the chair. You never asked."

"So you *do* want to talk about this now," he says, and his shoulders curl as he slumps and walks back into the room. "And there I was, keen to see your new chair and..."

"Avoid the subject?" she asks. There is a slight twitch around her eyes, it could be nervousness or fear for what she may soon hear. Or there could be a mote of dust – goodness knows there's plenty of it around in that room.

"Shall we invite *them* in to hear this?" he asks as he sits back down. He does not sink or collapse into the chair. It is a slow and controlled descent. He does not ooh or ah or exhale as he sits. He gestures towards the shrouded front door, at which point they both notice that the burbling murmur is ongoing, has never stopped, but had become part of the background noise, heard but not heard, registered but ignored – and without their knowing it or willing it.

"Would it make them go away afterwards?" she asks.

"I doubt it," he says.

"Then let's not," she says. "Not this time anyway."

"Okay," he says.

They sit and look at each other. They hear the murmur again. They listen to the creak and the tick and the hum of the house. In the kitchen, the fridge pump kicks in.

"You never asked," she says.

"I think you've already said that," he says.

"Why have you never asked?" she says.

"Because I don't care," he says. "It doesn't matter to me. I do what I do because it's what I *should* do. Because of who you are. Because... it's one of the commandments, isn't it?"

"But I want to tell you," she says. "I've wanted to tell you and you never... *you never* give me the opportunity. I want you to hear what..."

"I don't care," he says and he is interrupting without raising his voice. "It doesn't matter. I don't know what *they*'re expecting to gain from being out there but it's not going to be any great soul-baring from me because there's only one thing I can tell them, which I won't, and that's the way I feel. I might not agree with everything in that ancient book..."

"You hardly agree with any of it!" she says.

"Maybe so," he says. "But it says that I should honour and care for you. Of course I'd do that anyway. You carried me for nine months. You fed me and held me and comforted me in the night. You never told me to shut my eyes to keep the monsters away. You stayed with me until I could shoo them away on my own. You made me ready to face the world. You always, *always* had faith in me. You told me I could do anything I put my mind to and, let's face it, that wasn't true and isn't true but just that thought can carry anyone through all manner of mishap and setback and disaster. What else did I get from that book? Love the sinner while you hate the sin? If you read that the way I read it, it doesn't even matter if the sin happened, didn't happen or happened differently to the way you think it happened. I can't abandon you and won't abandon you and you can tell me if you like but I don't want to know and, if you force me to know, it won't make any difference to the way I feel so why bother? That's what I'd *tell* them. Do you think they'd *print* it?"

He gestures more wildly towards the front door, as though summoning some magical force and hurling it through the black-out curtain to the door and beyond, where it could swirl around the pack as they munch and chatter and wait and flirt.

And then, all of a sudden, there is some real news.

Even from the lounge, they hear a revving and a squealing and a thumping and a screeching and a crunching and a thudding.

Then they hear the sound of running and shouting.

Then they hear nothing but the breathing of the house.

She looks at him, wide eyed.

"No you don't," he says. "Correlation is *not* causation."

"Oh come on," she says. "Let me enjoy the thought just a little while longer. They'll be back, won't they?"

"Oh yes," he says. "They'll be back. But, before that happens, shall I put the kettle on? For once it'll just be for a cup of tea."

"Yes please," she says, "but tell me one thing before you go."

He pauses in the doorway and turns.

"You made up that story about the monsters, didn't you?" she asks.

"Does it matter?" he says. "As long as everything turns out all right in the end?"

Oswald and Victor

In my quieter moments, I write verse.

When the red box has been turned out, its contents digested, some replies drafted, some notes made in some margins, the awkward matters put off for a sunnier day and then the whole lot swept up, dropped in, lid clicked shut above it – then the tightening abates and the breathing is easier.

And I take the old fountain pen and a clean sheet of smooth heavy-stock paper and, whisky in left hand, I construct lines and rhymes, syllables skipping over the meter.

After a bad day of being patronised by the twerp, I write lousy limericks.

> *There was a ghastly toff called Oswald*
> *Whose colleague, called Victor, was quite bald*
> *One day Vic saw red*
> *Then Oswald was dead*
> *And into a shallow grave was pulled.*

Today had not been that bad. We had a slight falling out over who was responsible for announcing the new policy to ease the sacking of those suffering from long-term sickness. My, how the burden of regulation can stifle the relentless march of the corporations! But in the end we agreed that Lynne could have that particularly joyous potato.

He made eye contact. He appeared to be attempting to pay attention. His reasons for ignoring my views were marginally more cogent than I have been led to expect by recent experience.

I had gone home at a sensible time, the sun still squarely in the sky rather than dribbling over the horizon or long departed out west. It was not even low enough to trouble the chauffeur, some way from finding the sweet spot between visor and tree line.

The house was quiet. Given that I now live alone, that was not unexpected but was still unwelcome – the adjustment process will probably not complete in my lifetime. Mindfully peeling, slicing, chopping, stirring, drizzling my dinner into life, I was simultaneously prompting the radio interviewer. I was willing her into skewering her guest thoroughly – and, as ever, disappointed when she chose not to chase him through his loophole, to expose the dead end into which he had argued.

We should not be allied to these people but it is better to temper their wilder excesses than to snipe, powerless, from the benches on the far side of the house – although shouting at the radio often has as much effect as arguing with them in person.

With little in the red box demanding attention tonight, I made a long-delayed foray into the garden. The glimmering of evening light in the sky promised perhaps an hour before it would become too dark to work. The weeds were established but strenuous gardening is my exercise, sooner that than mingling with the braying idiots sweating into their iPod armbands. I confess that I occasionally personalise the work, especially when putting my hands around the weeds' necks and wrenching and pulling and twisting until their limp bodies are lying beside me.

But one cannot give in to mindless aggression and so I temper the activity (and grant the southern weeds a temporary reprieve) by pruning, shaping and even, on this warm evening, a little planting. After several years in a pot, brightening my patio, it was time to move the camellia into the bed. I would miss her but she would have to make her way in the world. And by looking just a little further down the garden, I could still enjoy her colour and vivacity.

Perhaps the trowel would have been sufficient but I had brought the large garden spade and fork and was vigorously breaking the soil with the tines when I was startled by an intruder. Unfortunately, it wasn't a burglar.

"Hello, Vic."

I recognised the voice. I didn't need to turn around. I knew who had interrupted the most rewarding work I had embarked on for several days.

"Good evening, Oswald. And please call me Victor – it always feels like you're talking to someone else if you call me Vic."

"I'll try," said Oswald Bourne, unwisely attempting a smile, "but I always think of you as a 'Vic'. And maybe you could call me 'Oz'?"

"I don't think I can. Did I leave the front door open or did one of your entourage credit-card the lock?"

"Yes, I'm sorry about sneaking up on you but I did ring the doorbell several times. Then I thought, you're always such a bore about your garden and when I saw the side gate was open..."

"No it wasn't."

"It *was* open. Or at least it was once I'd reached over and slid the bolt. Terrible security, Vic. You need to get a crime prevention officer round."

"Didn't you cut funding for them last week?"

Oswald's smile stretched slightly too far. "I think Lynne did that. She is so keen to please."

I finally stood up, hands on knees, slow straightening of the spine, slightly disconcerting crackling somewhere in my ligaments. "But you didn't come here and break into my garden to discuss crime prevention. Are you here for a while? Shall we go in and would your bodyguards like a cup of tea?"

"Just me tonight," said Oswald. "Thought I'd be safe popping round to see you. Just wanted to give you the heads-up that we're reshuffling Lynne out of the department."

"What?" I said. It possibly came out rather louder than I was expecting. "She's been your human shield for nigh-on eighteen months and this is how you reward her? I can't allow this, you're undermining me yet again and making Nigel seem ridiculous. I'm sure Nigel will take it to Duncan."

"Oh, Nigel's quite onboard. And Duncan's always happy to let me run my own ship. She's damaged goods."

"Only because you damaged her." I may have still been speaking rather loudly and there could have been a little theatrical spit in my voice. Perhaps his mixing and mangling of nautical metaphors was the outrage that drew out the extra volume.

Oswald seemed unsettled that I had abandoned the niceties of coalition coexistence, to such an extent that he tried to respect my personal space for a change. He did this by stepping backwards and, in so doing, trod on my camellia. She perished under his leather-soled shoe, her trunk crushed and broken, her roots denuded and helpless, her pot rolling slowly on the lawn.

"Oswald you cretin, will you watch where you're going? Isn't it enough for you to kill off economic growth in this nation without also preventing horticultural growth in my garden?"

I suppose it was quite funny with hindsight and with detachment, neither of which I was able to

Everything Turns Out Just Fine

access at the time. It certainly made Oswald laugh until I struck him with the spade and then the laugh became a clang and he made some very strange noises. I am not proud of what happened next, although history may show that it was the correct course of action.

A u-turn, the common approach of Oswald and Duncan, was certainly not an option and, now that I had begun, it was difficult to see how there could be a viable plan B.

The following morning, my hands were blistered, my back was aching terribly, my camellia was not dazzling me with either her voluptuous flowers or her fronds. Several shrubs on the northern border had been redistributed.

The hypericum was neither straight nor showing its best side. The abelia and buddleia had both been stripped of leaves, branches and flowers down one side as though they had been uprooted, left lying on their sides and then, perhaps, dragged across the hard, dry soil before being restored to the ground.

A better day at the office followed. The unexpected absence of Oswald Bourne had allowed progress in negotiations – subject, of course, to his approval as and when it would be declared from his perch on the mountaintop and dispensed to his supplicants. Lynne's self-respect blossomed. A very slight fall in unemployment enabled financial experts to declare green shoots of recovery.

Oh caryopteris your blue buds stare
Mournfully over lawn to your soulmate
Fuchsia standing, heady flo'ers hung in shame,
Blood red colour suckéd from blood-soaked soil.
Fallen soldiers feed their gaudy display
As on cent'ry-old battlefield she grows.

It is merely a hobby. I am not attempting to rival Shakespeare's use of limping iambic pentameter. And, sadly, reality was not living up to the poetic optimism. A recent addition to the soil was proving highly toxic. Dramatic wilting was occurring, which neither watering, nor feeding with the strongest and most mature of my garden compost, could reverse.

The public appeal for information went out on the day that I wrote off the buddleia, bagging it up for landfill rather than green-waste recycling since I could not risk its having become a carrier. Mr Bourne had asked his chauffeur to let him out about a mile from his home. It had been a balmy night and he had wanted a walk to clear his head and to order his thoughts. Had anyone seen him on his way home? Was anything suspicious spotted that night in the area? Could anyone furnish any lead at all?

I hadn't seen anything suspicious that night, of course, since I was at home for a good hour before Oswald bade his chauffeur good night. Even though I live a mere couple of miles from his home, or perhaps a single mile from the drop-off point, I would hardly have heard anything from either my kitchen or my garden. Had anyone asked, that would have been my answer. Occasionally, I wonder about triangulation of mobile phone signals and whether his route could still be plotted. Perhaps he had turned his phone off, the better to allow his head-clearing and thought-ordering.

The royal-purple-leaved smoke bush, despite claims of its thriving in poor soil and maintaining a magnificent colour throughout the summer, took grave exception to being asked to stand in for the expired buddleia. Flopping its leaves and branches down onto the ground, it seemed determined to leave the plot by death if not by pity of the gardener.

And so, finally, I have removed all plants from a good area of that border, replanting where possible, disposing where the ghost has clearly been given up. I unrolled tough turf over the area, shaping the edges into hyperbolic curves before stamping it down and watering.

As the policy reviews roll through the autumn and a compassion returns to the edicts issued from the department, as the replanted shrubs recover before bowing to the season, a shape begins to form in my newly extended lawn.

As the leaves turn golden and swoop and flop to the ground, a patch of brown and collapsing grass appears. It is about as long as a man's body, about as wide as a man's chest in its centre, with narrow branches spreading from each side, together with two thicker branches reaching out from one end. From the other end, a brown shape, about the size of a football is darkening, this area being the furthest gone.

> *A poisonous man would best be contained*
> *So that his influence could be restrained*
> *To slaughtering the grass of a lawn*
> *And thus save those not to the manor born.*

> *For his passing no great number did mourn*
> *And now this new economic dawn*
> *Its sole cost a bald patch on my lawn.*

I dare not dig out the cause and, it seems, I cannot cover it with fresh growth. The thought of artificial foliage or decking appals me. And so I will brazenly ring the affected area with stones of many and various colours and lustres and, by drawing attention to it, will normalise its presence.

It will be the memorial to the fallen soldier. I will research the battles fought in this corner of the county and I will pick a long-forgotten army to commemorate. Ideally I will discover a battle won by the underdog, at great human cost, which led to a resurgence of quality of life and ethics for the nation. A battle that, if remembered at all, is known as a victory for those seeking to throw off the shackles of oppression and to restore hope to this green and pleasant land.

Palm Reader

When Madame Douard pressed his forefinger firmly onto Stella's collarbone, his little finger fluttering over and around the blouse buttons, she knew he was no ordinary palm reader. To be fair, she had already become suspicious.

The fair was squarely targeted at nostalgia junkies, having not moved with the times, having retained all the old rides, with their creaking wood, with their new paint slathered over the old, with the texture of the peeling layers adding faux grain to replace that long hidden by bright tawdry colours.

Oversized cuddly toys leered over the coconut shies.

The central box office sat under its haze of cashier's cigarette smoke, guardian of the paper and metal money, dispenser of the plastic tokens.

And over in one corner, set up against the railings of the park, by the bus stop but a good couple of hundred yards away from the gate, was a burgundy pencil-shaped tent with tie-dye detailing, streamers of glittery plastic leading from its pointed summit to the ground and three sets of wind-chimes. Curly block capitals on a simple blackboard described the services on offer.

MADAME DOUARD PALM READINGS
FORTUNES TOLD LIVES REALIGNED CASH
ONLY NO REFUNDS

Stella had seen the tail-lights of her bus disappear over the hump-back bridge. It would be at least thirty minutes until the next one. The bus stop was little more than a subtle accessory worn by a lamppost – it had no shelter, no seat, not even an advertising poster to divert her. Her phone's battery was nearly flat and was being reserved for emergency calls. It could not be wasted on chatting, emailing, texting, internet browsing, ebook reading or Angry Bird launching.

Doing nothing was utterly unthinkable and so there was no other choice. It took some minutes to walk up to the park gate and pick her tottering way across the damp grass almost back to where she started. Another woman was now standing at the bus stop. She looked up at Stella and half-smiled when she realised what Stella was about to do. Stella smiled back, a thin mind-your-own-business smile, then turned towards the tent.

The fair was quiet – perhaps unlikely to come to this suburban green again – but this corner was deserted. Even the plaintive calling of the coconut shy man was muted at this distance. Madame Douard's tent flaps were closed. There was no sound from within.

Stella looked again at the blackboard. No prices

were displayed. Stella opened her handbag. There was no one around, no need to worry about urchins or footpads jostling her as they rummaged through her make-up and wet-wipes, grasping for valuables. She opened her purse. She decided how much she was prepared to pay. Then she decided how much more she would be prepared to tolerate because otherwise it would be disappointment, failure – and going back to waiting for the bus. And she might have to have a conversation with the other woman. And this smiling, newly-arrived woman had that look of desperation in her eyes which made Stella worry that it would be a long and fraught conversation that she, Stella, would have little part in except to be cast as 'sympathetic listener'. Stella was not a sympathetic listener.

Stella grasped the tent flaps, called out 'knock knock', and pulled them open. Smoke and an astringent incense vapour caught at the back of her throat. Her eyes began to water, she coughed inconveniently and a warm hand took her hand. A figure in a cloak, partially obscured in the darkness (oh, the cliché, she thought), led her to a chair. She sank into it.

"Cup of tea?" he asked. He paused. "Nothing funny, not any of that herbal muck, just a good cup of British tea to sort out that throat."

There was no getting away from the fact that Madame Douard was a man. Stella briefly considered the possibility that the good lady had a husky voice but the beard was the clincher.

"Thank you. That would be lovely," she said. "I mean, I wouldn't normally take drinks from strange men in smoky tents but I figure..."

"...that it's a long wait for the bus and what harm could it do?" he said, smiling as he turned to her, holding a floral china cup nestled into a nearly-matching saucer, complete with jauntily-angled digestive biscuit.

"Thank you," said Stella. She paused while unbuttoning her coat and opening it, pushing it back on her shoulders but not shrugging her arms free, ready for a sharp exit. "But you already had this waiting. It's as though you..."

"Predict the future, like a fortune teller?" said Madame Douard. He strained his mouth as though trying to smile without realising in time that he was already doing so.

"No," said Stella. "As though you make them every so often on the off-chance someone will come by. If they do, it's a great trick, a wonderful opener. And if they don't, you have a cup of tea."

Madame Douard's smile wilted but did not fade away completely. "That is mere supposition!" he said, waving his arms in a gesture reminiscent more of guiding an airliner to the gate than dismissing a spurious argument.

"And there's only one cup," said Stella.

"Okay. Busted," said Madame Douard. He sat down on his chair, a basic wooden affair suited to the worker, not the customer – a stark contrast to the weary yet soft and welcoming dark-blue armchair enveloping Stella. The table between them wore an off-white tassles-and-lace tablecloth, partially protecting it from candle-wax. Three decks of cards, not quite in neat piles, were to one side. Stella couldn't tell if they were for tarot, conjuring or patience.

"Do I need to eat the biscuit as well as drink the tea before you can pour out the tea leaves?" asked Stella. "Or should we agree the rate before I do any more than sit down?"

"Never mind the rate," said Madame Douard. "Wait till we're done. And then, if you don't feel it was worth every penny, don't pay me"

"Satisfaction guaranteed?" asked Stella. "You could add that to your sign. It would go nicely with 'NO REFUNDS'. And..."

"You're going to ask about the 'MADAME' bit on the sign, aren't you?"

Stella sighed. "You really can't claim any special powers for guessing I was going to ask about *that*," she said. "What's the matter with using your real name? Did you think a male palm reader wouldn't be successful? I don't mean to be cruel but you hardly seem to be getting a queue of customers this way either."

"But that is my name," said Madame Douard.

"Your name is 'Madame'?" asked Stella. "Really?"

"No, it's Adam. But I am French. And 'M' is an abbreviation for Monsieur. And my surname is Edouard. And that is what I wrote. It's not my fault if you misread the spacing." He crossed his arms and tilted his head back a little, as though adopting a Napoleonic stance. "But let's not talk about me, Stella, let's talk about you."

"Okay, Adam," said Stella, then her forehead creased slightly. "Good guess on my name. I won't ask how you knew because Sherlock routines leave me quite cold. So how do we start?"

"We could start," said Adam, "by working out why Sherlock routines leave you cold. Imagine that you have a fridge."

"I don't have to imagine," said Stella, snorting slightly but adding a cough to the mixture in an unsuccessful attempt to disguise the contempt, "because I have a fridge." She pulled her coat squarely back onto her shoulders.

"And imagine," said Adam, "that your fridge has a temperature dial marked with numbers between zero and six."

"Mine has a proper temperature scale on it," said Stella. "How is anyone supposed to know what those numbers mean?"

"But just imagine," said Adam, a slight edge of irritation briefly crisping his consonants, "that you have one of those cheaper models. Where do you set the dial?"

"Three, obviously," said Stella without the

slightest pause. "Then turn it up or down a bit if it needs adjusting. Not that I'd know which way meant colder but it wouldn't take too long to discover which one it was."

"Exactly!" said Adam. "Everyone's a three. And that's where everyone goes wrong."

"If that's the best you can do, I don't think we're going to agree on the fee," said Stella, but with a smile on her face before she raised the cup to her lips.

"You've got to push at the boundaries," continued Adam. "Be a six. Be a zero – find out which is best, don't accept mediocrity."

"But Adam," said Stella, "that could be good advice in real life – but in fridge-life you'll either have frosty food or mouldy cheese."

"Mould is *good* on cheese," said Adam a little too loudly. "In fact, would cheese have been discovered if it hadn't been for people keeping milk in warm conditions?"

"I don't think you really understand where cheese comes from, do you?" said Stella. "There's a little more to it." She put the cup down on the saucer carefully. They were not from the same set and the base of the cup didn't quite rest easily in the saucer's groove. "Is it okay to put this down or are you about to do a trick with the tablecloth?"

"I am *not* a conjurer," said Adam, flattening the smile from his mouth, looking Stella directly in the eye, constructing a fair attempt at a serious look. "I am asking the preliminary questions so that I can tell which approach to take. I think I have determined that. And please put your cup on the table. "

He stood and walked behind her. Stella kept her gaze on the table, resisting the itchy urge to turn her head and find out exactly what he was up to. He was probably rummaging in a suitcase. First there had been the sound of the catches clicking open. Then the slight waft of air as the lid opened had fluttered the candle flames and rippled the hair hanging over the back of her neck. Then there was a plastic bag rustling sound, before the suitcase lid was swung closed with a whoosh and the resulting small spatter of candle-wax on the tablecloth.

And then his forefinger was on her collarbone.

"You know that's not my palm, right?" said Stella. "But you have lovely smooth fingers."

"Just moisturised them," said Adam. "And lifelines aren't just in palms, you know. The ones near the heart can tell you much more."

"I bet they can," said Stella. "Just watch where you're going with the other fingers."

"Excuse me!" said Adam. His hand was gone from her skin but he did not walk back in front of her. "What sort of operation do you think I'm running here?"

"I'm sorry," said Stella. "No, I really am. I'm just nervous and you standing behind me has got me on edge."

"And that's intentional," said Adam, "but if I'd told you that and told you what I was going to do then I wouldn't have had the element of surprise – which is very important."

He walked back around her armchair, turned and sat in his chair. He straightened the crease in his trousers and looked up.

Stella had slumped, her chin resting on her chest, her eyes either closed or looking down. Her hands had been resting on her lap but one began to slide and, suddenly, slipped over the side of her thigh, the arm hanging limply and swaying slightly.

"Stella?" said Adam.

"Boo!" shouted Stella, jerking upright and throwing her arms forward, all jazz-hands and twitchy elbows. "How's that for the element of surprise?"

"Oh Stella," said Adam. He sighed. "We could make progress here and I know you have to work through the ridicule but I can..."

"Get me on the right track?" said Stella, smiling as her hands slowly made their way back to her lap. "I just wanted my palm read, just a little diversion while I waited for the bus. I never asked for the new-age life-coach routine. But thank you for the tea. I've left the biscuit."

"Left the biscuit..." said Adam.

"You're not going to make some terrible pun about that really taking the biscuit, are you?" said Stella. She smiled, but it was a small smile, the sort she would normally use on a very young child who had finally managed to use the correct end of the crayon.

"Okay, that's enough of the criticism," said Adam, and perhaps, again, there was a slight edge to his voice. "I'm trying to help you here and, frankly, I'm not enjoying your attitude, even though you probably think you're being playful."

He paused but Stella did not use the space to defend herself, make fun of him or change the subject. She was still, looking up at him, neutral expression on her face.

"I'm sorry that I don't have a magic wand on the table," said Adam. "I'm sorry that the trunk over there isn't a trap door into a mystical land. It's got a few spare robes which smell of Darjeeling tea because it used to be a tea chest and the smell really gets into the wood and doesn't come out. And there's some hand cream. I'm sorry that I don't have a fully functioning crystal ball. But I'm trying to help here."

"You're a palm reader who doesn't read palms – how much help do you think people are expecting?" asked Stella, eyebrows slightly raised, not a hint of mockery in her voice.

"How much were *you* expecting?" asked Adam.

"None," said Stella, shaking her head, looking intently at her hands which were crossed in her lap. "To be honest, I thought it might be a fun way to wait for the bus."

"And is it?" asked Adam.

"No," said Stella. She looked up at him. "Sorry."

"So maybe if you stopped making fun of me for a minute, we could see if that was better, couldn't we?" said Adam.

"You sound like you're talking to a child when you phrase it like that," said Stella.

Adam said nothing.

"Okay, point taken," said Stella. "Carry on. I'll try to stay quiet and listen." She folded her hands more neatly in her lap then relaxed them again as though concerned it might be taken as a sarcastic gesture – or perhaps it merely turned out to be less comfortable than she had thought it would be.

"Thank you," said Adam. "I think you're like me. And I think that we're like the fridge. We're trapped at number three, which is okay but it's not getting us anywhere exciting. There's no frosty food or mouldy cheese in our lives but there aren't any snowball fights or cocktails on the beach either. And yes, I'm talking figuratively, not literally, so please don't tell me that you had a Sangria in Majorca only last month."

Stella shook her head, eyes wide, signalling no, not me, guv, I wasn't going to say it, honest.

"But it won't do," said Adam. "I use myself as an example. Don't end up like me. I'm not good enough at this to do well, I won't succeed. Clearly being a successful palm reader isn't a success anyway but my life-coaching skills aren't going anywhere either. But I'm too good at it to want to let it go. I don't mean I give good advice – how would I ever know anyway? Who ever comes back to tell me? What I mean is that I do it well enough for *me*. I enjoy doing this. I'm the customer, really. But it's not going anywhere."

"I don't see how..." said Stella, but she stopped and mouthed 'sorry'.

"You don't want to end up sitting in a tent wearing a cloak," said Adam. "Not literally, of course. But here I am and here you are and we're not so dissimilar and we can help each other to just break out of the rut and other clichés like that. Just because I'm trapped in this tent doesn't mean you have to carry on with what you have. Break free and express yourself and find..."

"Okay," said Stella. "Sorry but I can't stay silent any longer. It's all true but it's so abstract. I know this. Everyone knows this. But most people don't know what to do about it. And I'm not convinced you're going to tell me. And I don't even know why you put your finger on my collarbone. But I do know that my bus is coming in a few minutes and I've got to squelch my way back across the grass to get to the gate so..."

"Can I come with you?" asked Adam.

"Yes of course you can," said Stella. "But don't even think about keeping the beard. You know, my fridge might be a three but you're wrong about me. I'm a six all the way. Or a 'max' if that's what you get beyond six." She started buttoning her coat. "You'd better get that cloak off or people will stare. I mean it. Really. Everything is going to be just fine. And you can leave this tent any time you like, starting right now."

Adam's mouth was slightly open. "Nothing like this has ever happened before," he said.

"Have you ever asked before?" said Stella.

"No," said Adam.

"That's why it's never happened before," said Stella. "Now get a move on."

Adam's cloak turned out to be an overcoat – he merely hadn't put his arms in the sleeves. He pulled it around himself properly and opened the tent flap. "After you," he said.

"Thank you," said Stella. She picked up her handbag, left the tent and started across the grass.

"Hang on," said Adam. "There's a loose..." He pulled one of the railings sharply upwards until its base was clear of the lower bar. Then he pulled the base towards himself and slid the railing out. "After you," he said again.

Stella and then Adam climbed through the gap, ignoring the startled expression on the face of the lady who had now been waiting some time for the bus. She was partway through a telephone conversation and the look of desperate need for a sympathetic listener had retreated. Adam replaced the railing.

"It's about time we left," he said. "Madame

Douard would have been back any minute. I'm Dominic. I'd like to say I was the apprentice palm reader but actually I just saw that she'd popped out for a cigarette break and that you were coming over so I thought I'd just..."

While he was speaking, the bus arrived. It was the number six. The lady in less need of a sympathetic listener climbed on. Stella followed her.

And then Dominic stepped up and reached into his pocket for his pass and pressed it to the machine and there was a double-pip and the word 'CHILD' appeared on the screen.

"You can't use that," said the driver.

"Why not?" asked Dominic.

"It's a child's card. And you're not a child," said the driver. He kept his eyes front, scanning the road, not looking at his miscreant would-be passenger. Peripheral vision, apparently, sufficed to determine that Dominic was above the age of sixteen.

"Must have picked up my son's card today," said Dominic. "So he must have mine. Okay, how about I just bip it on the machine again? Twice child fare is adult fare, right?"

"You can't use that," said the driver again.

"Then refund the fare and I'll pay cash," said Dominic.

"I can't do that," said the driver. "Phone the helpline. Now please either pay or get off my bus."

"All right, all right," said Dominic, glancing up

the length of the bus in the hope of finding sympathy, support or just a friendly face. Stella had sat down near the back and was staring out of the window.

He patted his pockets but heard no jingle of coins.

"Oh, for goodness sake," he said, but lightly. "Stella, could you lend me a couple of quid?"

She didn't look up.

"Stella?" he said again. Again she didn't look up. He paused, not for long, but long enough to elicit a weary sigh from the driver.

Then Dominic smiled at the driver. "Actually, maybe the walk will do me good," he said as he stepped down to the pavement.

He glanced at the railing, at the park, at the fair and at his tent. Then he smiled, shook his head and turned to cross the road.

"Did you know him?" asked the lady who had been in need of a sympathetic listener. She was sitting in front of Stella, twisting awkwardly. "Only you seemed to leave the park together."

"Pardon?" said Stella.

"You knew him, didn't you?" said the lady.

"Oh yes," said Stella. "I've known him for years." She paused and stared off into the middle distance, perhaps looking out of the window at a distant figure crossing a road. "But he never remembers me. I thought, maybe, this time, as he knew my name, he might..."

"Yes?" said the lady, straining her neck even further around.

"But then he didn't," continued Stella. "Maybe next time."

Loved Their Jobs

Ready?

Ready.

We were somewhere around Tacoma near the edge of Commencement Bay when the phone began to take hold.

You've definitely stolen that from somewhere.

Of course I have. That's the whole point. It was originally about drugs. The drugs taking hold. It felt like that with the phone. Mark Prince. Over and over again.

You didn't have to answer it.

I normally didn't answer it. But it wasn't my phone. And I could hardly stop him answering his own phone. Especially if I was driving at the time.

Mark Prince. Reminds me that we had a Henry King at my school. Teachers used to love reading out lists of names, any excuse. Never tired of King, Henry. And when he was in eighth grade, that just seemed to goad them on.

Prince Mark certainly talked like he thought he was royalty. Anyone would think he was calling for something urgent, instead of just being unable to sell the re-branding to the client by himself. It wasn't that he didn't have the new catch-phrase...

Don't they call them strap-lines?

Do they?

Or slogans?

Does it matter?

Not to me.

Me neither. So it wasn't that he didn't have the usual list of examples – first there's the one they like, which the client won't, but they'll try to convince them...

They'd try to get the client to buy something they're confident he won't like? Doesn't sound like a sensible way to do business.

Well everyone likes a challenge. Maybe it's a test to see if the client's awake, or to see just how good they are at sales.

Not convinced. Carry on.

Thank you. Then there's the one that the client will definitely like but which is a bit dull and too similar to the last campaign...

...which is the one they'll go for, so presumably there isn't a third?

Oh yes there is. There's the final, sacrificial one that no one likes and everyone can be happy rejecting. It means they end up agreeing with each other. Smiles, slaps on the back, that sort of stuff.

Do they really work like that?

Jim told me they did. But maybe it was just him that worked like that. Anyway, dear Prince Mark couldn't cope with talking to the client without running through everything with Jim first. In excruciating detail. And often through areas of very poor mobile phone reception.

He had given Jim the time off, right?

Probably hadn't wanted to. Typical incompetent middle-management leech.

That's not fair, is it? Some of my best friends work in middle-management.

No they don't.

Well, some of them have friends who do.

We're going off on a tangent.

We always go off on tangents. I want to tell my side of it. You're taking too long.

Only because you keep interrupting.

Which I only do because you're taking too long. So Doug was supposed to take me away that weekend.

Tell them where.

I was just about to. We were going to catch the ferry from Prince Rupert to Skagway. I was looking forward to the whales.

And the view?

Of course the view. But the whales – it was the right time of year for them or something.

Or something?

And you accused me of interrupting too much?

Sorry.

But that morning, we're packed, we're ready to go, the phone rings, Doug talks to Rowan. And suddenly Doug's not feeling too good and can't face the drive, or the days on the ship. But it's nothing that Rowan said to him – no, of course not. But Rowan would like a little help and as he's not up to the trip...

...he'd be healthy enough to sit in the office for a couple of days staring at a screen and just tidying up a few things?

Yep, that was pretty much how it went. And then it got really weird.

These people already sound quite weird enough.

You know this story already. Stop annotating.

Annotating? What happened? You swallowed a thesaurus to get ready for this interview?

Yes, Paul, that's exactly what I did. So I'd been cooking the eggs but I'd just stopped while Doug was constructing this elaborate excuse to get out of the trip and get back to the office. And the egg was starting to catch, you know, the way scrambled egg sort-of browns and curls. Just thinking about it, I'm smelling it right now. That burny-eggy smell.

You're sure it's just a memory?

Shut up and don't be gross. So I said something like, 'I wish you'd fixed this cooker hood when I asked you to then I could use it right now to get this smell out of here'.

Didn't you put a sweary word in there, between 'this' and 'cooker hood'?

Probably.

Bit of a clumsy sentence, isn't it?

It was something like that. I don't know if I've

got all the words in the right order.

I hope you haven't. The subordinate clauses are crying out for their own sentence.

I'm sorry, I didn't realise I'd dialled the grammar helpline.

We'll get you a good grasp of English in the end. Now, carry on with the story.

I think I'll ignore you for a while. So... I said that sentence which apparently is a bit clumsy. And then the fan sort of coughed and spluttered and came back to life. And Dougie, dear Dougie, said something about my wishes being granted that morning.

Seriously?

Yes, seriously. And, again, you know this story already. So I said, well, if I've got three wishes...

Why would you assume three wishes? Okay, maybe that's the global standard for fairy tales but...

But nothing. They don't exist except in fairy tales. And, since Dougie was going all fairy tale on me, I thought I'd play along in the same genre.

Genre?

Yes, genre. You got a problem with me using the right word?

No.

Good. So I said, if I've got three wishes, I'm not going to waste any more of them on appliances. I'll wish for a long healthy life for everyone I love and for evil to be punished.

I like this bit.

So then the radio programme gets interrupted by some newsflash about that evil bloke being found by some soldiers and thoroughly and comprehensively shot to death.

As opposed to shot to life?

Shut up. So we heard that but I didn't jump to any conclusions.

Surely even *you* wondered for a moment.

Wondered what? Whether I had a hot-line to some great, ancient power? Come on, Paul. Repeat after me... correlation is not causation. Post hoc ergo propter hoc.

Where did you get that Latin one? You didn't throw that one at me last time.

Look it up. Just because something follows something doesn't mean...

...it caused it. Yes, I know. But still, you must have felt a bit funny about it, surely.

I thought it was *funny, as much as anyone being brutally killed can be funny, but I didn't* feel *funny about it. But Dougie started saying, how come two of your wishes came true but not the third? And I said, what are you talking about? And he said that I'd wished for long healthy lives for everyone I loved but that he was still feeling not too good.*

He was *that* non-specific? Not too good?

He was that *non-specific. And I just stared at him. And he blurted out that it just showed that I didn't love him. And I couldn't think of anything to say to something that bone-headed but unfortunately I laughed and that just really got him wound up.*

And up till this point you hadn't realised he was an idiot?

He is not an idiot. I must have hit a nerve.

Jugular, more like, and not before time. Oh, and he is an idiot. I've met him. I'm entitled to my opinion.

It wasn't a normal meeting.

You're right it wasn't! I couldn't believe that a grown man would start chasing me around my car.

Why didn't you just stop running away from him?

It's all very easy for you to say, now, sitting there. But I was the one being chased by a man with an expression that I can only describe as looking like murder. And I thought he was an idiot. And idiots can be dangerous.

Lucky you had a big car.

Lucky I had the full insurance deal. You know I lied about that mirror?

The one Doug hit with the...

...the baseball bat he was chasing me with?

No he wasn't. It was his umbrella.

It was a baseball bat. Why had he even brought it with him? What did you tell him?

It was an umbrella. So what did you tell them about the mirror?

I said I came back to the car in a car park and found it smashed. They seemed happy with that.

Like I said, I had the full insurance deal. As long as I brought back something that looked like it could once have been the car, they'd be happy enough.

Why didn't you tell them the truth?

What? Why didn't I tell them I was being chased around a car by an idiot with a baseball bat?

Umbrella!

Baseball bat! And why didn't I tell them about how I got in and locked the door and he then hit the mirror with the bat? Yes, let's think... Why didn't I tell them that? I'd still be explaining it – that's why I didn't tell them. And they'd probably have asked me to ask the police to talk to Doug and then he would probably have said it was an umbrella...

You can still smash a mirror with an umbrella.

Of course you can. But you don't want inconsistencies in these stories, do you? Makes the whole thing sound suspicious. And it sounds like you would have backed him up.

I wouldn't have said he hadn't broken the mirror!

But you would have said it was an umbrella.

It was *an umbrella!*

See? And once you've put doubt into the story, they would have wondered whether any other part was wrong. And then your dear Doug would have tried to make it sound like it was my fault.

You might have a point. But I don't think Dougie would have lied.

Oh, he's Dougie now, is he?

He's always been Dougie. Just because we're not together any more – doesn't change his name.

So would you have backed him up if he'd said it was an umbrella?

It was *an umbrella!*

Ah yes, you remember it well. You'll tell me next that I was dressed in gold when I was all in blue.

I have no idea what you're talking about.

The song! You know, the one that goes 'ah yes, I remember it well'.

Not really. Modern, is it?

Twentieth century, yes.

First or second half?

Yes. The first or the second half. Probably the middle half. How would I know? Then there's that lovely line, 'Am I getting old? Oh no! Not you!'

I feel I'm getting old listening to you sometimes. But where was I?

We were talking about my little meeting with Dougie, when I came back to yours to help you pack up your things.

No we weren't. We were still at the bit where Doug thought I had superpowers but that he was still feeling ill because I didn't love him enough.

It doesn't sound any better phrased like that than it did earlier.

I'm not sure how I could make it sound any better.

Just say he was an idiot.

Maybe. You're slowly convincing me that he

might have been.

Have been? Surely he still is?

Happily I wouldn't know for sure whether he still is. So, by the end of that conversation, he'd convinced himself, and me a little bit, to be honest, that I never really loved him. And that I should go on the trip. And that he would seriously think about what should happen when I came back. And that I should too.

I'm surprised you went.

I'm glad I did.

So am I.

Really?

Of course!

I'm just messing with you. It was close. It seemed a ridiculous thing to do. Romantic trip for one? But that look on his face. I just wanted to get away from that...

Idiocy?

No.

Insanity?

I wasn't going to say that either but... Yeah, pretty much.

Jim used a different 'I' word on me. Called me immature.

Cutting!

Yes. I think there might have been a 'selfish' and an 'unrealistic' thrown in for good measure. Apparently I needed to respect his job but he didn't need to respect the fact that it was my holiday too.

He actually said that?

Not directly. But he managed to change the subject when I pointed out it was my holiday too – and that just because he'd sold his life, soul and whatever else to some bunch of pen-pushers, it was hardly fair to expect me to play along. I mean, it's not like *I* was going to get a larger bonus for screwing up *my* holiday the way he thought *he* was going to.

And did he?

I never asked. I hope it was about as big as a book of stamps. The half-dozen size, not the full dozen. Oh, but he did say that Prince Mark would *probably* pay my airfare home too.

What were you supposed to do about that 'probably'?

I never asked. Because I didn't fly home early – remember?

Oh, yes. That'll be why you were on the ship when I met you.

So there we were. On the ship. I remember you driving your wheezy compact onto the car deck, while I was parking the ludicrous, oversized 'dump it on the foreigner' rental car. That heap of junk was so stupidly long it actually cost extra to put it on the ship. I never *realised* how long it was. You park end-on all the time so you don't notice just how much *car* you're driving around with.

You didn't walk around it before you took it off the rental-car lot? You know, kick the tyres, check for anything damaged by an umbrella or baseball bat? Maybe felt tired once you'd done a lap and wondered why that was?

No, not really. It was only the following week that I tried to parallel-park it against the kerb and noticed that most of the spaces were too small.

Before or after you'd hit a few cars?

Funny.

Careless of you to take a car you couldn't drive properly.

Yeah, thanks. I'll know for next time. So there we were, both of us staring at grey smudges and wondering if they were whales a *seriously* long way away or just dirt on the window.

Why weren't we outside? I honestly can't remember why I would have been trying to whale-spot inside.

Remember the wind?

Yes, that might have been it.

And being outside would only have made the whales a few yards nearer. We needed them to be about a quarter-of-a-mile nearer.

Do they ever get that near to the ships?

Maybe the tourist ones sail over to them. We were on a ferry. You can't expect it to do everything that the cruise ships do.

I just thought that spending a few minutes going a bit off course...

No. That's not what ferries do.

And you've studied all the ferries ever, have

you?

You're just being silly.

Of course I am. I thought that was what you liked about me.

One of the things.

Can you think of any others?

Probably. But there's something even more important that we need to think up. The changes.

What changes?

Exactly. We only get this published if we can come up with something heart-breaking or tear-jerking or chin-scratching about how we changed or were changed or changed someone else. You know, the glossy-magazine personal-interest article climax. What did we learn from this?

Don't spend time with people you don't like much?

I don't think that's going to satisfy them. How about we start them off with a warning against going on a long, heavily-planned trip with a workaholic who'll bail out if his bossy-wossy yanks his chain?

That trip was heavily-planned? Firstly, what does heavy planning look like? And secondly, all you did was book a couple of flights and set yourself a challenge of making it from the first to the second. Is that really your idea of planning, let alone heavy planning?

Okay, drop the heavily.

Thank you. Yeah, that's a good opener. But we'll

need more heart-ache and conflict. You could talk a bit about the airport.

Oh yes. That's the second step. Or maybe the one-and-a-halfth step. Don't drive a bailing holiday companion to the airport. Let him figure it out for himself.

Was it really that bad?

I think the cop was wondering whether to go for his gun.

You're exaggerating.

The shouting got quite loud. And that's 'quite' in the American sense.

Thank you for that.

You're welcome. He was complaining that I'd got him there too early and what was he supposed to do with the extra three hours and I pointed out that I had a boat to catch and couldn't waste time taking him on a half-day jolly. And that if he didn't want to spend three hours in the airport, he could just *come with* and get the flight he was already booked on, going home in ten days.

Risky. What if he'd said yes?

He wasn't going to say yes. And if he had, it would have been fine. He's a bit of a teenager, really. Massive stroppy rows then complete amnesia-style business as usual.

And?

Yes, I'm pretty much the same so it would have been fine. But it wasn't going to happen. And it didn't. And it just got louder and louder. Me

shouting, I mean. I don't think he'd heard me lose it
like that before.

*I don't think many people have. Is it really
scary?*

I hope so. Wouldn't be much point in doing it if
it wasn't. Yes, I slightly told him what I really
thought and went back through many years of pent-
up stuff which I thought I'd put to the back of my
mind to forget about. Turns out I was just saving it
all up for a special occasion. Like this one.

What's the story with the cop?

I'm not sure. I think maybe we were sitting there
too long, in the drop-off-only place. Maybe he
thought it was suspicious that no one had got out of
the car.

Why didn't Jim just get out?

I don't know. Maybe because he had three hours
to kill and thought that listening to me shouting at
him would be more fun than staring at the wall in an
airport.

It'd be close, I imagine.

So I'm shouting, Jim's looking at me like *I've*
gone strange.

You had.

Okay, I had. And the cop's standing outside
shouting and then he raps on the glass and I turn
and... Well, it cleared the air.

*You didn't get out of the car and freak him out,
did you?*

I wound the window down. And I kept my hands

where he could see them. I know the drill. I've seen the movies. And I smiled and apologised and, well, we hadn't actually done anything wrong.

He couldn't find anything to write a ticket for?

I guess not. Maybe he heard enough to realise that we were both being punished enough already.

And what did Jim say to you?

Nothing. He just took it with a little half-smile on his face, then the cop came along, then we spoke to the cop, then Jim got out, took his bags, and went. Didn't look back.

You stayed long enough to know he didn't look back?

I was blocked in by a taxi.

Really?

I don't know. Probably. But he didn't look back, which I guess I know because I was looking at him so maybe I wasn't blocked in. Then he was inside the terminal. Then he didn't walk back for five minutes.

You waited five minutes? You never told me that before.

I was blocked in by another taxi. Then I left.

I think you're right.

About what?

That the first thing we learned was not to take a trip with a workaholic. And definitely not to drive them to the airport if they want to leave early.

Okay, and then there's the other thing. The thing we learned together.

You want to tell people about that*?*

No, not *that* part. I was thinking more – don't assume you'll spend the rest of your life with someone you meet in a cafeteria on a car ferry, even if there's a good view out of the window with whales and all?

I think most sensible people would know that already.

But would sensible people be reading this sort of drivel? This isn't for them. This is for people who think it's going to be a heart-warming tale of love over adversity.

But it is! Everything turns out just fine in the end, doesn't it? You didn't outstay your visa...

I didn't have a visa. There's a visa waiver scheme and...

No one cares. So... no problems with immigration, neither of us spent a fortune on anything silly like a new home or a flashy ring or...

You know, I regret that I didn't get you a really special gift but...

You did. Your friendship. Sorry – was that a bit much, even for our target audience?

Who knows? Wait for the letters of complaint to come rolling in. And you found another guy – actually, he's called Guy, isn't he?

No. That was the previous, er, guy. My husband's Ed. You know that. You met him. He's not an idiot. He never chased you round anything while holding anything.

That's most people I meet. You know, Doug really was one of a kind.

I still see him occasionally. Have I told you that? Pushing a pram. Or was that a few years ago? Can't remember how old his twins are. Or was it just the one? I find it harder and harder to remember or care. He looks at me like a man struggling to remember his own name, let alone the name of the person he's looking at.

Like a cow at a passing train?

You've stolen that from someone, haven't you?

You're not answering the question because you know it's true and you know that proves that Doug's an idiot.

I think you steal all your best lines. You definitely stole that first line you used on me.

Do you still remember what I said?

I don't think I'll ever forget it.

Go on – prove it...

You said...

Yes?

Shut up. I'm just trying to get into character. 'So – you also here on your own because the guy you thought you were going to travel with decided he loved his job a bit too much?'

Was I really that clumsy?

Probably worse. I'm sure I've tightened up the phrasing. Do you remember what I said back?

Yes. You said 'yes'.

I said more than that!

No you didn't.

I said something like, 'I guess we both loved people who loved their jobs'.

No! That's pretty good but you've invented that afterwards. You just said 'yes', then you asked me about my accent, then we had a few drinks and then we didn't stop talking for about a month.

I didn't invent it afterwards. And it was six weeks.

That's about a month.

We should have stayed together.

It wouldn't have worked.

We should have tried it for longer.

It was a rebound. And I rebounded back home and you rebounded off Guy and onto Ed. And I'm...

Yes?

Still looking.

What are you looking for?

I'm looking for someone like you. But a someone like you who's looking for a someone like me.

I was looking for someone like you.

Was?

Was.

Not 'is'?

You mean 'am'. No. Definitely 'was'. And you were the one who said it wasn't working.

It wasn't. And it wouldn't have.

But now you think...?

The same. Which is why I'm looking for a someone like you who's looking for a someone like me.

There'll be a someone. It's a big world...

...with plenty of fish in the sea?

I wasn't going to go there – but... yes. You're not getting upset are you?

No.

It's so hard to tell over the phone. Are you sure?

Yes. I think we're done.

Really? Have we given them enough?

I don't care. That's how much they're getting. You want to sum up?

Not really. Can't we leave it there?

I'll do it then. Here goes.

I'll add the drum roll in post-production.

Thanks for spoiling the mood.

Don't mention it.

Okay. So, here's the summing up. I'm happy we met. And it would never have happened without Doug and Jim. I guess, looking back on it, they weren't the only ones who loved their jobs. Even though, God knows, we didn't realise it at the time.

Thursday's Child

The pacing was subtle but detectable. It was the sound of a man who did not want to sit still, who had no need to rest, yet who did not want to appear impatient. Footfall after footfall with a break in rhythm at each end of the room as he turned.

"Won't be long," called Ed.

He heard an uh-huh or perhaps an mm-hmm. Through the door it was difficult to tell the difference.

Ed couldn't remember the man's name. There had been so many parts to it, each with a story and a reason – and he had sat and nodded as the man had spun the tales. He knew that part of it meant Thursday because he had thought at the time that Thursday's child has far to go and how appropriate that would be, even though it was a completely different mythology. But, working his way through the rhyme of aphorisms to get to Thursday, he couldn't remember Tuesday's line, which bugged him and, as he failed to think of being full of grace, his attention had lapsed. There had definitely been a sentence in there somewhere that had included the words "but call me..." although he had not the slightest idea what had followed that phrase.

He would think of the man as Thursday and try not to call him that to his face – or through a closed door for that matter.

It was a lie anyway. He *would* probably be some time. Whether it had been the ice in the drink, the fish, the vegetables, the rice, brushing his teeth with tap water or just something that he had picked up another way (was there another way?) – it seemed irrelevant right now. He picked up one of the bottles of mineral water. He didn't recognise the name – why should he assume it was any better than what came out of the tap? He had no answer to that question but took a sip from the bottle anyway. It couldn't make things any worse.

Maybe Thursday was being passive-aggressive. Quiet footfalls making more impact than huffing, tutting, precise stamping. How far was this man prepared to walk?

And as Ed stared at the wall, his phone rang – not the hotel phone but the phone buzzing gently in his pocket that had been stationed by his left ankle for quite a while now. This was when Ed realised that he had become the sort of person who would answer the phone wherever he was.

It gave a barrage of noise, thumps, chips, splintering and smashing before he heard Jim's voice cutting through.

"Hello, is that Ed?"

"Hi Jim. How's it going?" He tried to keep his

voice level and controlled but he couldn't disguise the acoustic.

"Sorry, I've caught you at a bad time, haven't I?" said Jim.

"No, I was just..." said Ed.

"You're not in the hotel bathroom then?" said Jim. "I can call back later or you can..."

"No, it's okay," said Ed. "Tell me what you need."

"Well," said Jim. "Your walls. Not good. Too thin to hide the pipework, too much blockwork to shift the studs, too much..."

Ed found himself looking at the wall nearest to where he was sitting. He knocked his fingers against it ever so gently and felt the unflexing, reassuringly solid construction. And yet, in his technologically-advanced, resolutely first-world, quality-driven home country, walls could be made out of little more than cardboard stretched across a few thin planks around randomly placed breezeblocks. Mind you, at least he could put up a picture at home without using a hammer-action drill. He hadn't, but he could if he wanted to. Whether it would stay up was another question entirely.

"So is that okay?" asked Jim, before another deluge of demolition sounds overloaded his phone's tiny speaker.

"You're the expert," said Ed.

"I'm the what?" called Thursday.

"Sorry, not talking to you," said Ed.

"Pardon?" said Jim through a distortion of white noise.

"I'm sure that's all fine," said Ed. "Does it make any difference to the price?"

"No," said Jim.

"And will it be done by the time I get back?" asked Ed.

"Yes," said Jim. "Actually, hang on – when are you back?"

"Very funny," said Ed. "Goodbye." And he hung up.

"You okay in there?" asked Thursday.

"Yes," said Ed. "Shouldn't be long now."

His friends had told him that he was making a mistake. Sitting staring at an unlovely wall, feeling the churning trumping his impatience to get going, to get out, to climb higher than he had ever climbed before (literally, of course – he didn't go in for any new-age mumbo-jumbo), he wondered if perhaps they had been right.

Having his bathroom refitted while trekking in Nepal might have been overly ambitious.

He couldn't count on being contactable if his choice of rustic matt-finish tile became unavailable. He wouldn't be on site to check that the bath had the tap holes drilled in the correct corner. And there would be questions (there are always so many questions) which he should answer himself, not leave to the random and potentially wayward discretion of the plumber, project manager or passing salesman. Questions about walls, on the other hand – *those* he was quite happy to delegate.

His thighs were going numb. His calves were suffering from pins and needles. There was a knock on the door – not the bathroom door but the main door to his room. He heard Thursday opening the door. He heard the sound of normal conversation, albeit in a language he wouldn't have understood even if the consonants hadn't been filed down by passing through the door, even if the vowels hadn't all been flattened into similarity by distance and hushed tones.

This was even more irritating than the pacing. He wanted to call out, to ask what was going on, whether it was anything to do with him, to say that he wouldn't be long (which was still a lie). He wanted to be involved in the discussion. But he really didn't want to have a protracted conversation from here. How to phrase it?

And then the conversation ended and the door opened and closed and the pacing started again. The second time that Thursday passed the bathroom door, he said, "They want to know when you're leaving."

"Leaving?" asked Ed.

"Yes," said Thursday. "Checking out. Should have vacated the room by now."

"Oh," said Ed. "What did you tell them?"

"What you told me," said Thursday. "That you

wouldn't be long."

From a sufficiently single-minded perspective, this whole adventure was due to someone *not going to be long*. If he wanted to construct a tenuous and somewhat fragile timeline from this Nepalese hotel bathroom backwards to the single event that led to him being there, it would have to trail, floppily and unsatisfactorily, back to Jonathan calling him to say that he wouldn't be long.

To be fair to Jonathan, *he* had phoned *Ed* – Ed hadn't had to phone him. But it was still Ed who was sitting, *literally* twiddling his thumbs on a bench-seat in a chain, but fashionable, restaurant, while Jonathan finished whatever work it was he had blamed in a vague fashion and ambled (he had no other walking speed) around the corner to where Ed was wondering whether he should at least order a starter to absorb some of the drink.

And during the working or the ambling or perhaps the co-worker flirting, the man sitting facing Ed, at the next table, the man who had been fiddling with his phone (as men do in restaurants and indeed any and every other venue), turned it around to show to the woman sitting with her back to Ed. This gave Ed a clear view of the screen. So Ed saw precisely what was fascinating to the man and was about to be engrossing for the woman. It was a photograph of Ed.

It wasn't a photograph of her, with him in the background. It wasn't a photograph of the room, with Ed's face inadvertently captured. It was a well-composed shot, using a little zoom to show Ed's face in the upper two-thirds of the screen with enough neck and shoulder to look the way a portrait has traditionally looked ever since artists discovered that they could dispense with drawing difficult details like too much shirt or elbows or knuckles. Or, for that matter, work out how best to represent the motion of thumbs rotating around each other.

And now Ed had the terrible middle-class anxiety of what he should do about it. Angry confrontation, friendly conversation, passive-aggressive ignoring while giving *the eye* – he could have discussed this with Jonathan if only Jonathan had *turned up*. Although if Jonathan had turned up, the man wouldn't have had a clear view of Ed's face so the situation probably wouldn't have occurred at all. Yes, on reflection, it was definitely all Jonathan's fault.

And then it got a whole lot worse when the man *noticed* that Ed had noticed and smiled and got up and came over.

"Sorry," he said. "You don't mind, do you? You must get this all the time."

"Er," said Ed because that really wasn't even close to what he was expecting the man to say. "That wasn't even close to what I was expecting you to say."

"You were expecting me to ask for an autograph?" asked the man. If there was any sarcasm or mocking in the voice, Ed was unable to detect it.

"Not really," said Ed. "No one has ever asked me for an autograph before and I didn't think that would start today. And no stranger has ever taken my picture before either."

"I apologise. I thought you were someone else."

"But who did you think I was?" asked Ed.

"Doesn't matter," said the man. "More importantly, I am sorry that you've never been photographed by a stranger before. That must mean that you've never done anything extraordinary in your life. Sorry for taking up your time. I'll delete the picture."

And the man turned away, returned to his seat and, holding up the phone so that Ed could clearly see the screen, he pressed the little picture of a dustbin and the picture of Ed's face was electronically crumpled and sucked into it. The dustbin's lid wobbled in a way that the programmer had probably considered cute.

"Wait a minute," called Ed.

The man shrugged. "It's gone," he said.

"No," said Ed. "Tell me – it does matter – who did you think I was?"

And before Jonathan arrived, Erik sat at Ed's table for a few minutes and told him about the mountaineer that he resembled so dramatically. He told him about the man's remarkable triumphs and his courageous failures and his indomitable spirit.

He really used the phrase 'indomitable spirit' – Ed
assumed it had come from the authorised biography
although, when he bought it later that day and read
it over the course of the following week, he didn't
find it anywhere.

What he did find in *The Mountain Man – An
Authorised Biography* was the great man's
suggestion of a starter peak. There was no
endorsement, no recommended route, nothing
actionable in case of injury – just a throwaway one-
liner about how, if he was starting again, right now,
with none of his life experiences but a burning
desire to stand astride the summits of the world, he
would seriously consider doing that one first.

Ed threw money at the problem. He had plenty of
it and didn't have any great interest in training, or in
spending hours of his life scurrying up and down
the climbing wall at his local leisure centre while
being gawped at through the large show-off window
by passers-by. The thought of scrambling up local
mountains, those only a few hours away by car with
ample parking and marked routes and single-file
tourists jostling for space on the crowded paths –
that was not his style at all.

Instead, he turned to the internet, found a
company with a good flashy website and no
negative reviews on the first result page that Google
produced – and told them what he needed and asked
them how much. They negotiated the fee, they
agreed the terms and here he was, living the dream,

sitting on a toilet in Kathmandu with a man called Thursday pacing up and down outside.

He had an appointment with Erik – and he had every intention of turning up, on time (not like Jonathan, curse him) and with photographic proof of his triumph. He could do something extraordinary too. And then Erik could damn well take another photograph of him and he would be worthy of it.

Just as soon as the stomach cramps subsided.

Ed had never understood why pain had to be so competitive. His relationship with Guinevere never fully recovered from his offhand remark about heartburn (or getting a stitch while running or some other trivial matter) which earned him a broadside diatribe about how nothing, *nothing*, could compare to the life-changingly profound pain of childbirth. His mild response that he had, in no way, suggested that it was comparable seemed to make matters far worse.

By nature, Ed was a decent, open, warm individual – it had to be true because it had appeared on his CV for the last twenty years. However – and he was aware of this and working on improving it but finding that the harder he tried, the worse it got – people thought he was sarcastic.

"You're looking great," he would say to a friend, such as, perhaps, Guinevere when they used to be able to converse.

"What's wrong with the way I look?" she would

reply with the haunted look of a hunted and possibly fatally wounded prey.

"I said I thought you looked great," he would say, smiling.

"Yes, but you said it with that tone and *that* smile," she would say.

And yet, before the perceived sarcasm and the profundity of childbirth, she had loved him and he had loved her. It had to be true because they had said it to each other while looking each other in the eye. And they had also said it as an optional extra couplet inserted between prescribed lines in the wedding vows – it had been heard by the witnesses at the ceremony and by the congregation sitting smiling encouragingly from the pews. It had probably been recorded by someone on a video camera. (Back then, camera-phones were still a badly-performing luxury.)

Now that *was* a time when he had done something extraordinary – but the only stranger photographing him was being paid to do so by Guinevere's parents. He didn't think that really counted.

There is nothing but praise and support and talk of courage at the joining of two people into a state of holy enshacklement. But the grit and determination and, yes, the courage required to admit defeat, to say that they'd given it a good try but that it clearly wasn't working, and to say that merely clinging on for the sake of societal expectations wasn't going to cut it – that courage was never fêted.

But he wasn't climbing the mountain to show Guinevere or to give Gwendoline a reason to be proud of her daddy. If he had really wanted her to be proud of him, he would have absolutely insisted that she couldn't possibly be called that and made sure she didn't grow up with a name like a dead weight.

He wasn't even climbing the mountain as a retort to Erik.

But his mind was wandering. He was waiting for the stomach cramps to abate and, just for a moment, as he was off along memory lane (amnesia lane, more like it), the pain faded away. And returned as soon as he thought he was starting to feel better. He needed distraction. He needed to feel it was safe to get up and start moving, start travelling, start climbing.

Maybe not quite yet.

It was quiet outside his bathroom. The pacing had stopped.

"Er... hello?" he said. He would have called Thursday by name if only he could have been certain what it was.

"Yes?" The reply sounded like it was coming from very close to the door.

"Are you standing right by the door?" he asked.

"Yes," said Thursday. "You hadn't said anything for a long time. And I hadn't heard any, er, *sounds* for a while either. I was checking that you hadn't fainted."

"I haven't fainted," said Ed.

"Well obviously I know that," said Thursday. "What can I help you with? Would you like me to start carrying the luggage downstairs?"

"Not yet," said Ed. "I was actually hoping that you might... this is going to sound ridiculous."

"I doubt it will be any more ridiculous than some of the things I've been asked to do before," said Thursday with, as far as Ed could tell, a smile on his face. "Tell me."

"Yes, tell me," said Ed.

"Tell you what?" asked Thursday.

"Tell me about some of the ridiculous things you've been asked to do before," said Ed. "I was going to ask you to tell me a story, to tell me anything that can distract me."

"Distract you from what?" asked Thursday.

"From the pain in my guts," said Ed.

"Ah, I see," said Thursday. "Does it need to be a happy story?"

"No," said Ed. "Just anything interesting and distracting." He paused. "I can't feel my ankles."

"I can't feel them either," said Thursday. "Have you heard the story about Dorian Bale?"

"No," said Ed. "But what shall I do about my ankles?"

"Rub them," said Thursday. "Dorian Bale was left alone on the side of a mountain by his climbing party. They wanted to get to the summit. He wanted to sit down for a rest. They knew it was altitude sickness, that his thoughts were no longer lucid."

"So they heroically carried him back to base camp, right?" asked Ed.

"No," said Thursday. "They discussed it. Right in front of him, they discussed it. He *agreed* that they should carry on – not that his agreement in that state was worth anything. But they thought that he knew the risks. They agreed that his *failure* shouldn't stop them achieving their dream. He agreed to that too."

"Is this story going to have a happy ending?" asked Ed. "Someone spoke up and objected and used phrases like 'being able to live with myself'?"

"No," said Thursday. "They all accepted that he would almost certainly perish if they left him. But that is precisely what they did. They followed their dream."

"Really? All of them?" said Ed. "So they moved on and he died?"

"No," said Thursday. "Don't be so pedantic."

"I wasn't," said Ed.

"And please be less sarcastic," said Thursday. "It'll help us get along. So my party found him. And every person in my party insisted that we help Dorian. They knew they wouldn't get to the summit that day or, in all probabilities, ever if they stopped. But they stopped."

"Wouldn't anyone?" asked Ed.

"Thirty-seven people went past us," said

Thursday. "Some of them even put on funny accents and pretended they didn't speak English. I speak a lot of languages but they didn't seem to understand simple requests for help in any of those languages either. And his party not only didn't stop but actually abandoned him – don't forget them in your honour hall of fame."

"There's definitely more sarcasm in your voice than mine," said Ed.

The phone rang. Thursday stopped talking. Ed took it out of his pocket.

"You going to answer that?" said Thursday.

"Sorry," said Ed and stroked the phone's screen. "Hello Jim."

"Ed," said Jim. "Sounds like I'm still catching you at a bad time."

"Doesn't matter, Jim," said Ed. "If you're phoning me, I'm assuming it's important because I did ask you to only phone me if *it was important*."

"Steady," said Jim. "Just needed to get your go-ahead. Because it could be expensive. You see, your bathroom floor, it's not what we were expecting. You wouldn't believe what they've done. Instead of..."

Ed didn't really hear much else. The odd word or phrase cut through, such as 'polystyrene foam', 'load bearing' and 'concrete'. But Ed was still with Thursday's story, somewhere between fifteen and twenty thousand feet. And with low oxygen, temperatures around minus-ten and travelling companions prepared to take neglect all the way over to manslaughter, the choice between ceramic and vinyl flooring seemed trivial. Against the overall cost, an extra few hundred wasn't going to matter.

"That sounds fine," said Ed. "I'm happy with that option."

"I gave you two choices," said Jim.

"Which one would you pick?" asked Ed. "I'll have that one."

"Okay," said Jim. "Do you want to choose the..."

"Gotta go," said Ed. "I'm up a mountain." And he disconnected the call and turned the phone off.

"So what happened?" he said.

Thursday had restarted his pacing. If only he'd paid more attention, he could call him by name. Honestly, he really ought to have worked out manners by his age.

"What happened on the mountain?" he said.

"Oh, I didn't realise you were talking to me," said Thursday. "Off the phone now?"

"Yes and I've switched it off," said Ed.

"Good," said Thursday. "But can't we finish the story out here or..."

"Won't be long now," said Ed.

"I thought you might say that," said Thursday. He sighed. "Where was I?"

"Some number of people walked past and didn't help you," said Ed.

"That's right. But we got him back down. He

lived. Fingers and toes not necessarily all present and correct in the long term. But he hadn't been a concert pianist before he went up the mountain so it was no great loss that he wasn't one when he came down either."

"And?" asked Ed.

"And what?" asked Thursday.

"Isn't there some moral to this?" said Ed. "It's really not a satisfying story without some sort of forgiveness of his original party or them being haunted by their actions or..."

"What do you want?" asked Thursday. He sounded slightly angry. "Some people are horrible. What else do you need to know? They insisted that they hadn't done anything wrong, proudly showed everyone the photos of themselves at the summit and carried on with their lives. Mr Bale made another attempt the following year. Successfully too. But then he went with a better team."

"You?" asked Ed.

"Yes," said Thursday. "And people I trust. Decent human beings. Great mountaineers too. But I won't climb with people unless they're both. Funnily enough, Mr Bale's planning another trip with the original charming bunch. I won't be accompanying him on that one."

"Hang on," said Ed.

"That's what I'm doing," said Thursday. There might have been a smile in his voice. It was hard to tell.

"I'm not a great mountaineer," said Ed, "and you're climbing with me."

"Yes, but we're not climbing a mountain," said Thursday.

"Pardon?" said Ed.

"We're not climbing a mountain," said Thursday. "I'm sorry – is that a surprise to you?"

"Well, er, *yes*," said Ed. "What do you think I'm doing here?" His voice was getting ever so slightly louder, each word's consonants becoming progressively more brittle.

"What do *you* think you're doing here?" asked Thursday. "Because you're sure as hell not going anywhere near anything dangerous or technically difficult. We're going trekking."

"I specifically said I wanted the summit view," said Ed.

"And that's what you're getting," said Thursday. "Honestly – did you look carefully at what you booked? Did you really think a reputable firm like mine would take a novice all the way up?"

"Yes," said Ed. "Summit view – that's what I booked and paid for. The view from the summit."

"No," said Thursday. "The view *of* the summit. And we get the angles and perspective perfectly aligned so that it even looks like you're standing up there. Bit of zoom, bit of crouching and no one would know the difference."

There was silence from the bathroom.

"It's the classic fake shot," said Thursday. "Even

some of the pros use it if they're on a tight deadline. There was some bloke writing a book who did that a few years back. Looked a little like you, now I think of it. Can't remember his name but he said he was going to use some title like 'man of the mountain'. I thought it sounded daft but I just kept nodding and smiling. People seem to like the nodding and smiling. Also, dropping prepositions, not using the word 'the' and generally sounding like I've only been speaking English for a few weeks."

Ed still had nothing to add.

"I don't do this because I'm a hick," said Thursday. "I've got a degree in PPE from Oxford but I happen to like mountaineering, and the money's okay if you want to live here, which I do. Incidentally, you think my name's Thursday, don't you?"

Ed only said, "Sorry, yes... Sorry," but he suspected that Thursday knew that his eyes had widened and his jaw had dropped open before he spoke.

"Yes, you're the sort who doesn't pay attention," said Thursday. "I told you to call me Karl but I could tell it hadn't gone in. Here's what you need to do. Have a trek, enjoy the adventure, get your photos, show them to Erik. Wallow in your new bath. Apologise to your wife and reconnect with her. Cherish your daughter. Apologise to her too. Drop the sarcasm. Pay more attention. You might think my name is Thursday, but you're the one with far to go. It's not too far but try to do it full of grace."

"Thank you, Karl," said Ed. "That all sounds like..."

"Never mind what it sounds like," said Karl. "Trust me. Everything will turn out just fine. But you *will* need to come out of there before the sun goes down."

Other Homes

After a good look-around, some peeking and a little prying, she moved upstairs. It was the logical thing to do next.

She had run her finger along the spines of the books, sighed at the primary-coloured self-help, tutted at the potboilers, considered planning a mini-break with the guidebook promising charming, family-run hotels. Her glance had flicked up and down the CD-rack, taking in the strangulated tenors, yelping divas, youthful mumblers – nothing recent, possibly due to musical disaffection, more likely embarrassment-proof download-only.

Merely casting an eye over the *covers* in the magazine rack had been distressing enough – the ridiculing of minor celebrities unable or unwilling to spend *enough* money battling the ageing process, or too grounded (or too *poor*) to just send someone else out on the supermarket errands. At least she had never faced that level of scrutiny.

Most of the saucepans had dusty handles. The single frying pan still sported its cardboard show-off hey-look-at-me insert, easily enough torn out before a first use that clearly had not yet come. Be fair, she thought, they might have bought it yesterday. A small stack of foil-packed, plastic-filmed, soi-disant gourmet meals occupied the centre of the fridge; a few punnets of processed fruit sat below, divested of those inconvenient skins and stones and pips, some pieces slightly curling, some gaining in texture as the moisture left and was whisked away by the fans or evaporators or whatever voodoo these fancy machines used now to prevent the dependably slow-motion condensation waterfall down the back wall.

The winter coats were still hanging on the hooks by the door. The coat cupboard was full of ironing board and clothes airers and vacuum cleaner and bleaches and polishes and mop and bucket and brushes and dusters.

A single cobweb hung tight in the corner, cocooning the burglar alarm motion detector – easily disabled, code is 1812, like the overture, like the older kid's birthday, you know, eighteenth of December.

She turned off the bathtap, the last few drops skittered and spattered onto the foam mountain that had formed below. A slightly steamy heat haze wobbled across the ripples. She stopped and stared and considered and then pulled out the plug. The moment had passed. She didn't really *feel like it* any more, even though she felt childish for giving way to the change of mind, for accepting the slightly scuzzy unwashed feeling as normal and, just this once, honest, as *okay*.

And some tune that she once knew (or maybe once *sang*) came to mind and, before properly deciding whether she wanted to hear it or wanted it to lodge in her ear, she was humming it. The words were something about a bath or water or bubbles or some other inconsequential teenager-pleasing piffle – but set to a catchy tune.

As she crossed the hall, she imprecisely remembered the thrill of her mother taking her to friends' houses for the first time and that magical phrase of "why don't you show her your bedroom?" and having a look at the wallpaper, the posters, the curtains, the toys, the games, the gadgets, the trinkets. As an adult, it was rare to even make it upstairs unless, of course, it was going to see what her granny would have called a *special friend* and there had been precious few of those recently. Could there have been a little spring in her step as she crossed the threshold? Surely not – this was supposed to be a little nose-around, not scurrilous thrill-seeking. Maybe she was holding her breath a little.

There was nothing worthy of excitement in the bedroom. Mismatched furniture, shoe-induced scuffing low to the ground on the bedstead, a book next to a lamp on a bedside table. Hang on, that's the book she was reading. It was *his* side of the bed – she deduced this merely from the functional blue tissue box contrasting with the floral cube-shaped box on the other side. Which bit was he up to, she wondered, striding across, picking it up, flicking through it to find the bookmark, dropping a small slip from somewhere in the middle.

Uh oh.

She should pick it up. That's right. She should pick it up and put it back. That's what she should do. Under no circumstances should she look at it and read it and wonder about those numbers, those six numbers printed on the front. Well, looking at the numbers wasn't so terrible, was it? And it wasn't like anyone was going to know she'd looked – but then she absolutely mustn't pull her phone from her pocket and go to the website and see whether and, oh Jesus, all six numbers match and what now?

What now? *Really?* This murky water was certainly not difficult to successfully navigate. It didn't take her long to put it back in the book, between what she hoped were the correct pages, and to replace the book where she had found it. She never did check which page he was up to. Somehow it no longer seemed important.

Debra had kindly said that she could use their bathroom for a *nice hot bath* – she had actually stipulated that it should be *hot* and that it could be *nice* – while her boiler was being dismembered on the front lawn and while its successor was being enthroned in the little cupboard behind the little door in the corner of the kitchen. This was day three

of the work, if she allowed her definition of the
word 'work' to loosen sufficiently to encompass
arriving mid-morning, deciding that a component
was missing, declaring that it could not possibly be
obtained until the following day, requesting, starting
and finishing a cup of tea and then departing. And
so, for the third morning, she was here – not for
privacy but for hot water which did not have to
come from a kettle.

Clearly, having a root around was a minor
betrayal of trust but it paled into insignificance
compared to absconding with an IOU for a king's
ransom and heading for the nearest airport with a
flight to a country without a solid extradition treaty.
Besides, her passport had less than six months to
run and some places would be funny about letting
her in.

So *they*'d be moving soon. It would have been a
wonderful opportunity to snap up a home at an
estate-agent-free price if it wasn't for the fact that
she already owned an identical property next door
without a damp patch or an ugly pastiche fireplace
(below a damp patch) – and her shrubs were so
much more colourful across a wider swathe of the
year. Having both would be greedy – yes, that and
financially impossible.

The people who remembered her would be
surprised. "Financially impossible?" they would
say. "Surely a trivial sum," they would say. But
people who remembered her were few and far

between those days. The passage of time had protected her privacy – she hadn't been photographed for such a long time – and the girl in those old pictures was not the grey-haired lady who was spending her afternoon rifling through the neighbours' bedside drawers.

And there, in Debra's bedside drawer, was the business card of the police sergeant who had led the investigation. Having police officers dishing out cards like tawdry hawkers at a trade fair felt wrong and demeaning – look at their lovely *logo* and the way it says *Police* in an important way – and yet, what else would she expect them to do? Tear a piece of paper out of their notebook and doodle a phone number with a chewed ballpoint pen? With hindsight, the story of Debra's brush with the criminal underworld was hilarious although it was probably a little soon for Debra to see it that way.

Debra had come to her afterwards for the delightful cliché *tea 'n' sympathy* combo and she had provided a willing ear and a nod and an uh-huh and even some oh-yesses.

Debra had known *those people* for *so* many years and the kids had played together and the invitation to a fortnight in their villa – just get your flights and don't worry about the rest – had seemed so delightful.

Clearly the groundwork had been laid for years, what with the food fads and the places where they could and couldn't go to eat and how lovely to be invited but really they'd have to host because you couldn't trust the animal feed or the mercury in the fish or the GM in the wheat or the nuclear fall-out from wherever it was.

And so, after nearly a decade of fuss (and apology for fuss), the idea that their dear, long-standing, generous friends might want to ship their own favoured supply of meat to foreign climes seemed utterly normal and reasonable.

And, what's that? You can't fit it all in your own baggage allowance? Of course we'll take it for you, deep frozen and triple-wrapped and festooned with ice-packs. Well here's the suitcase to take it in and let us know if there are any extra charges or if you need a larger taxi or anything. Or something.

Looking on the bright side, the 'frozen meat carrier as drug mule' scam was at least discovered in dear old England, thereby removing the risk of execution that might have hanged over them (as it were) had it been uncovered at the other end of the journey. The mismatch between lifestyle and employment status finally made sense – even after so many years of friendship it can still be difficult to ask whether the money was inherited or the proceeds of crime. (Ha ha! It *was* crime after all!)

Debra still baulked at the thought of the money wasted on flights not taken, for which no insurance payout was offered. Even though she realised that they were lucky not to have received a hefty slap from the long arm of the law and that, technically, they were smuggling a dramatic quantity of high quality, highly illegal merchandise, she *still* felt that the only victim in the whole sorry episode was her.

They never saw the Murdochs again. Ignoring the one, fairly sizeable, betrayal of trust, Debra still missed her friends and would not tolerate the thought that the entire period of their friendship could be construed to have been skilful grooming. They *wouldn't* have done that, *would they*? According to Debra's husband, Oliver, a different family had been invited out each year. He'd spoken to some of the others. There seemed to have been a pattern of meat-carrying. He had not told Debra that they were the only ones who got caught.

So it had taken a middle-class catastrophe for her to meet Debra and Oliver, the reporters knocking on her door, the police searching their house (which, presumably, included rifling through their bedside drawers). She came out of her house and actually spoke to her neighbour and introduced herself (first-name only, of course, to reduce the chance of suffering the horror of being *recognised*). She became a non-judging ear to them and they, in return, have now offered a *nice, hot* bath which she will pretend to have had and then thank them accordingly.

There was a knock at the door. She froze. What was the protocol? Surely people don't arrive unannounced any more? If there's someone at the door then it's a friend who's expected (in which case, why isn't *she* here?) or a tradesman (in which case, *why* isn't she here?) or it's someone peddling a scam. Unless it's the postman, of course. She glided across to the front bedroom, the guest bedroom, the place where guests can enjoy the street noise while struggling to get a full night's sleep. Without even the slightest twitch of the net curtain she saw the luminous colour of the courier's van and she felt the pain of her last attempted redelivery, or collection from the depot, like a stabbing into whichever of the upper or lower intestines would smart more. And she skipped across the landing and she bobbled down the stairs and she opened the door as the courier returned to his van from the house across the street and drove away, leaving her facing the man in the raincoat.

And then it got even worse.

"I know you!" he said, the smile of delight scrabbling across his face and setting off the eyebrow-lift of wonder. "I bought both of your albums."

"Can I help you?" she asked. She folded her arms then let them fall by her side. She had always insisted (still would, if the opportunity presented itself) on the microphone being on a stand. Then a good strong stance – one hand gripping the microphone, one hand gripping the stand – took away the stress of deciding where to *put* her hands which, even now, for her, was not a trivial matter.

"This is embarrassing," he said. "Seeing you has

made me completely forget what I was going to say."

"Yes, yes," she said. "But you could start with your name and why you're here. If this isn't a social call, presumably you haven't forgotten what your job is."

"I'm Iain," he said, "with two 'i's."

"Thank you," she said. "I assume you mean as in 'Banks' rather than drawing attention to your two blue eyes."

"Yes," he said. "Thank you."

"I'm Ruth," said Ruth. "But you seemed to know that already."

They shook hands. She was still just inside the house. He was still just outside. She was still blocking the door and not moving aside to invite him in.

"*And*," she said, "there were three albums. But thank you for buying two of them. Not many bought the second and, well, not even *you* knew about the third. Now, how can I help you?"

"Can I come in?" he asked.

"But why are you here?" she asked. "You know, conversations at the door with strangers aren't supposed to go like this."

"How are they supposed to go?" he asked.

"You're supposed to tell me why you're here and then I let you read the gas meter or measure up to redecorate the dining room or serve me with legal papers or whatever it is and..." She paused, hoping he would take the opportunity to interrupt. He didn't. She sighed and continued, "...and that's what a normal visitor would do."

"I'm here to read the gas meter," he said.

"No you're not," she said. "They have a uniform and a gadget, not a raincoat and an air of mystery."

"*Do I* have an air of mystery?" he asked. "That sounds good. Especially given my job."

"You're a spy, aren't you?" she said, smiling before suddenly thinking that, if she was right, he might now need to bundle her off to a secret prison in a faraway country. "It's the raincoat," she said, hoping that would defuse the situation.

"No," he said. He paused. "That is, I'm not a spy. I'm not saying this isn't a raincoat. Although I'd have to say that I wasn't even if I was. Why I'm really here, or my cover story if I actually *am* a spy, is..."

He paused again, this time long enough for Ruth to add a mildly impatient "yes?" before a car drew up and a woman leaned out of the window.

"Iain?" she called. "I thought it was you."

"Oh for goodness sake," said Ruth. "What now?"

"Hang on a minute," said Iain to Ruth before turning and saying it again to the woman in the car. He pulled a mobile phone from his pocket and sent his finger sliding and twirling across the glass, tongue poking out a little in concentration. A final finger stab, a digitised whoosh and the message was on its way.

"I'm sorry," said Iain to Ruth. "I really need to talk to Kylie for a moment."

"Kylie?" said Ruth. "There really are people called that?"

Iain shrugged. "Don't feel you need to stand there waiting..." he said.

"Oh believe me, I don't," said Ruth.

"I'll knock again in a few minutes, if that's all right," he continued.

"Whatever works for you," she said, turned around and closed the door. She leaned back against it and tried to remember what she had been doing.

She had been downstairs. And there had been the item in the bedroom which she *really* didn't want to think about again in case temptation overtook her. And she had already both run and dismissed the bath and, well, why was she still in the house? Mainly, at the moment, because the alternative was to leave, lock up, and get back into her own home without having another strange conversation with Iain. He wasn't the strangest fan she had encountered in her time. But he *was* the only one she had encountered in some number of years which she didn't particularly want to calculate but which was probably approaching twenty. Who was she kidding? More like thirty.

She turned to look through the peep-hole. He was leaning right into the car through the open window, having either an *intimate* conversation or just one that was private. Alternatively, one of them could be hard of hearing. Could she, if she was really quiet, if she was really quick, if maybe she acted the spy and was sufficiently *sneaky*, could she make it back home without another Iain encounter? She had had the luck or foresight or just good sense, on a day of bumbling around, to wear trousers – so stepping over the nearly waist-high nasty wooden fence between the front gardens should be easy. She wouldn't have to brush past him on the pavement. That's decided. She'll do it and...

Unfortunately, all of those plans then went out of the window when the woman started walking down the stairs.

"I'm sorry, I'm going, I haven't taken anything," she said. "Back door was unlocked. I didn't break in."

She sped up. Ruth moved towards her. They reached the bottom of the stairs together. This time, Ruth was face to face with a stranger she was preventing from *leaving*. They looked each other up and down, Ruth checking for anything the stranger might use as a weapon, the stranger estimating how agile an adversary she was facing.

"How dare you," said Ruth finally, the words forced out through a twist of indignation and certainly not requiring a question-mark as no answer would be needed. She took her phone from her pocket. "I'm calling the police and *don't* think you can stop me."

She fumbled the screen unlock.

"You don't need to unlock the phone to make an emergency call," said the woman. "Can we just talk about this first?"

But Ruth already had the phone to her head. "Police." She paused waiting for the next person to answer. "I'm standing in front of a burglar in my home, I mean my friend's home. Yes, she's in front of me. Yes, *please come now*." She gave the address.

Then she looked up at the woman. "Shove past me, grab the laptop in the kitchen and get out."

The woman looked at her. "What?"

"You heard me," said Ruth and, without another word, the woman was gone. Ruth was upstairs before the back door clicked shut. As it clicked shut, she was in the bedroom and, a few seconds later, she had shaken a couple of drawers out onto the floor and was making her way back down the stairs. The lottery ticket was pressed and curved around her left buttock.

And as she opened the front door, the kid on the bike, cycling along the pavement, stopped by the man in the raincoat, who was leaning through a car window, removed the phone from that raincoat's pocket and pedalled furiously away.

"Oi!" shouted Iain, "come back here, you little..."

"Of course he's not going to come back," shouted Kylie, if that *really* was her name. "Jump in and I'll go after him."

He ran around the car, shouted something that

sounded like "sorry" at Ruth and, with an over-revved gear scrunch, they were gone.

"I never knew I lived in such a hotbed of crime," she said, some time later, to the policeman, "although if the back door really was unlocked, I suppose they were asking for it." She put her hand up to her mouth. "Oh goodness – will that mean they can't claim on their insurance?"

"What makes you think the back door was unlocked?" asked the policeman. "Looks to me like it was forced."

And *something* happened to his eyebrow or the corner of his mouth and she looked at him and wondered if it was a wink and if maybe, just maybe, he'd *fixed* the door so that it would look forced and then that could go in the report and, if the insurance company sent someone, it would look good enough to them.

"Did..." she started.

"Yes?" he asked.

"Nothing," she said. "How about Iain's phone?"

"Ah yes," he said. "I think that was probably the biter being bitten."

"What do you mean?" she asked, but felt a lurch as though her subconscious told her gut what it had figured out before bothering to pass the message through to the cognitive function.

"Have you heard of distraction theft?" he asked.

She nodded.

"He's probably been going up the street, ringing

the door, talking to anyone he finds while your lady burglar goes up the street via the back gardens, breaking in as she goes. If I had to guess, I'd say that he texted her to tell her to leave this house alone because he recognised you – a kind gesture from a fan, if you like – but it was too late and she was already in. So she tried to get out again but, well, you know the rest. That's my take on it, for what it's worth. And the kid was probably an opportunist. Unless he was working with the lady in the car – but you said she knew his name, right?"

But Ruth didn't answer because she was desperately trying to work out whether there had been any clues about *which way* Iain had approached from.

"You said up the street," she said.

"Yes," he said.

"I have to go home," she said.

"I'll come with you," he said.

And they went through much of the same process again. He examined the back door and tried to secure it as best he could while recommending a locksmith. He took notes and he helped while she piled and sorted and he gave her his card before he left. The logo had changed very slightly, the angle of the italicized letters had been adjusted, presumably the better to imply forward-thinking, a leaning-in attitude but without suggesting imbalance or recklessness. He took her list and explained the unlikelihood of this and the improbability of that but that she would be contacted if there were any personal effects to be identified.

Her original vinyl albums (pristine sleeves, one careful owner), had been cracked when they had been knocked off their shelf together with a heavy vase which had landed on them. It was almost as though the person rooting around had been in a hurry.

And going around and around in her head was the thought that Iain had saved *Debra's and Oliver's* house from his thieving little friend because he thought it was *her's*. The one time in over thirty years that her fame, in and of itself alone, accomplished something – and it accomplished it for her neighbours. And *they* only lost the laptop which they had offered to her only the previous week saying that they were thinking of selling it and how there wasn't anything personal left on it and they just weren't sure what to do with the thing – which is why she'd told the thief to take that as cover. *That's* how considerate she had been shortly before pilfering their lottery ticket which, curiously, they had never mentioned – not on the day when they came home from work to a street of crime reference numbers, not the following day when they had dinner and sympathy, not the following week when they compared and contrasted their insurance claim forms. Oliver hadn't brought it up and, well, clearly *Ruth* couldn't. Maybe Debra disapproved and so he bought them secretly and maybe he didn't even know he'd won if he hadn't had a chance to check and...

She'd better look again.

And there it was. Six numbers on the little pink slip matching the six numbers in the fatuous ball graphics on the screen. Shame the date at the top didn't match as well.

It turned out that Oliver liked to buy tickets *this* week with *last* week's numbers. He would explain it to her several months later when the subject innocently came up. It was during a dinner party, they had finished their starter and Debra was clattering around in the kitchen and Oliver's friend David or Daniel or something like that, leaned forward conspiratorially and, in his best stage whisper, asked if Oliver still did his lottery *thing*.

Oh yes, Oliver said. And Darren or Dorian tutted. And Oliver explained that it was the best way of making sure that if you hit the jackpot you wouldn't have to share it with someone else because no one buys last week's numbers even though there's just as much chance of them coming up as any other combination.

Oh yes, he said again, the odds would be astronomic against getting the same numbers two weeks running but, once the first week has passed, that's already happened so you can disregard it completely and the odds are, etc, etc.

And that reminded him that it turned out the burglar had snaffled his ticket out of his book and what a disappointment that must have been if she'd recognised the numbers and then taken it to the lottery place. And Ruth consoled herself that at least she hadn't suffered *that* indignity.

But, after all that, maybe everything would turn out... if not fine, at least okay. None of her property was ever discovered but the local news found out about the once-famous person whose fan/burglar saved the wrong house, and how her records got broken, which was a shame because they were pretty rare now and certainly weren't available for download – hell, they'd never even been rereleased on CD. Of course, that didn't mean they were valuable but clearly of sentimental value to her. The newsreader didn't actually say "aww" but, frankly, might as well have done.

And, rather wonderfully and coincidentally, she found out that none other than Tom Jones (who she'd had such a crush on all those years ago and, truth be told, still did) had seen the story. Who knew that superstar singers watched the local news? And he had remembered her ("I remember her from back then, lovely lady, beautiful voice").

And, back then, he had thought of singing with her but had never done anything about it. Did she think it would be too late to do that now? He had asked it straight to camera and she had phoned the BBC and they said they would pass on a message and, well, you never know, do you?

Loose Ends

A few small doses of luck can be more useful than swallowing down a large clump in one go. Bethany was glad for the luck that it had been a warm day so she had wound down the window. She was glad for the luck that the car had rolled onto its side and not continued rolling onto its roof, or onto its other side. And she was delighted to discover that seatbelt pretensioners do, indeed, tighten seatbelts prior to a crash, prior to an otherwise nose-breaking airbag inflation, prior to an otherwise whiplash-inducing thrown-forward tossed-backward episode.

The car was lying on its passenger side and so, with a click, she unfastened her seatbelt, shoved her elbow hard into the airbag and pulled herself up and out of the car.

Bethany was also grateful for the luck that it wasn't her car. She assumed it belonged to Gabriel, since that was the only possible explanation for the GAB413L registration plate. She wasn't sure which number she would have used instead of the '4' to stand in for the 'R' but, since her main feeling about personalised plates was pity (with contempt running a close second), she wasn't prepared to spend much time thinking about it.

Gabriel must have been the man who had started the engine but then hurried back into his house for whatever it was he'd forgotten. Intriguingly, there were several books by Gabriel someone-or-other which had originally been scattered across the back seat and were now resting against the side window. They were all the same. Bethany assumed that Gabriel was either an author or an author's stalker.

"Are you okay?" called a man who had just crossed the road but now hurried back. His overcoat swung out behind him like a cape, the wind adding to the effect. The beard spoilt the superhero appearance. Superheroes never have beards, Bethany thought. Why is that? Do people *really* still think that children are scared of beards? What about Santa?

"Yes," she said, smiling and doing a twirl-and-curtsy to show the extent of her non-injury. "Not a scratch. No cuts. No bruises. Quite thirsty, though. Any good coffee shops around here?"

The man paused. "Don't you think you should wait with the car?" he said.

"Why?" asked Bethany. "It's not like I can help tow it away. And they'll get all the owner's details from the number plate. And I'm quite thirsty. I'm Bethany, by the way."

"Dominic," said Dominic. "There *is* a good place just around the corner. Shall we?"

And he offered his arm, elbow out, which she

took with a grin and they, well, there's no other word to describe it, they *sauntered* along the road and around the corner and into the café and on to the banquette seats facing each other across a booth table.

"How did you...?" said Dominic.

"Roll the car over?" said Bethany.

"Yes," said Dominic. "Didn't the other driver stop?"

"Which driver?" said Bethany.

"Of the other car," said Dominic. "Are you sure you didn't hit your head?"

"There wasn't another car," said Bethany. "I just wondered what would happen if you turned like so and accelerated like that and then braked like this and then..." While she was speaking, she twisted the imaginary steering wheel that protruded from the table and stabbed her feet into the imaginary pedals under the table and vehemently jerked the imaginary handbrake lever in the upholstery next to her.

"And at which point did it...?"

"I'm not altogether sure," said Bethany, and she grinned at him again. "It all happened so quickly. I might have to try it again and see if I can make more sense of it second time around."

"Back again?" asked the waitress.

"I just can't stay away," said Dominic. "This is Bethany. I think she needs something soothing. She's just been in a car crash."

"Oh don't worry about that," said Bethany, still

smiling. "Just a minor prang, as my Nanna Doreen would have said." She looked up at the waitress. "I'll have whatever he's having."

"And I'll have my usual, please, Janice," said Dominic.

"Of course you will," said Janice.

Holding the cup so close to her face that the steam swirled up her nose, Bethany said, "What I really wanted was a Mini."

"When?" said Dominic.

"That car," said Bethany. "I really wanted to try it with a Mini. Not one of the proper, old, blow-the-doors-off Michael Caine Minis. No – one of the new huge four-door Minis. I saw one the other day. They're bigger than you think they're going to be."

"How big do you think I think they are?" said Dominic, smiling.

"Smarty-pants," said Bethany. "And I *heard* that huge Mini too, chuntering along the street with its diesel rattle. And I realised they should have called it a Maxi. But they didn't, which was clever because the jingle kinda writes itself. 'Looks like a Maxi, Sounds like a taxi, Not British no it's German, Can't swim like Ethel Merman...'"

She was singing a tune that sounded recognisable but Dominic couldn't place it. And she was swaying a little from side to side, bringing the cup along for the ride, somehow not spilling anything.

"Come on," she said suddenly. "Time to go. Would you be a love and pay? I left my purse in

Gabriel's car."

"Ah," said Dominic. "I don't have enough money on me either. Really sorry I forgot to mention it. Who's Gabriel?"

"Never mind," said Bethany, standing up, turning and smiling at Janice who was slowly, methodically and drearily polishing glasses behind the bar. "Off we go. Just smile and walk and act like we've left the money on the table. It'll work out just fine. Here we go."

She took Dominic's hand and started walking and he followed not because she was pulling hard (because she wasn't), nor because she was gripping firmly (because she wasn't). And it took several hundred yards and a few corners turned before he stopped, and their arms went taut then slack as their hands slipped apart because their grips turned out to be even weaker than either of them assumed.

"I have to go back and pay," he said. "It's my local café. I go there all the time. They know me."

"Suit yourself," said Bethany. "But before you go..." She paused to make sure she had his full attention, that his eyes were locked onto hers, that any fingery fidgets or foot-tapping nerves had subsided. Then she carried on. "When you put on your shoes and found your keys and opened the front door and set off... what did you come out for?"

"Oh," said Dominic, eyes up, down, left, as though searching the immediate surroundings for the answer. "I came out for a pint of milk."

"No," said Bethany, and she really *did* stamp her foot as she said it. "What did you come out *for*?"

"I was looking for something different," said Dominic, looking at his feet but not finding anything different there.

"And did you find it?" asked Bethany, grinning at him and performing a slight bow.

"Yes," said Dominic.

"And are you going to follow the *something different* to see where it leads?" she asked, now cocking her head slightly to one side.

"No," said Dominic. "If I don't go back and pay, it'll come out of Janice's wages. And she doesn't deserve that, even though she's grouchy most days."

"Oh come on," said Bethany. "She'd thank you for it. For once she'd actually have an *excuse* to be grouchy. She could claim her previous grouchiness had always been because she knew something like this would happen. She wouldn't look happy but she'd *be* happy because she'd feel justified. Instead of just *feeling* that the whole world was against her, she'd have the beginnings of the *proof*. Imagine the satisfaction!"

"It's been nice chatting," said Dominic, "but I have to go now."

"Okay," said Bethany. "Suit yourself."

And, without a backwards glance, she stepped forwards and, without a sideways glance, she stepped into the road and, without even time for a squeal of tyres or a honk of horn, she rolled across the bonnet of the cautiously driven car that struck her, much to the stunned horror of the smartly-dressed man, driving his sensible car, wearing his trilby.

"Bethany!" shouted Dominic. He ran around to the front of the car, where she had dismounted the bonnet in the middle of the road.

The driver sat and watched.

Bethany had landed on her hands and feet, her knees and elbows bent to absorb the impact. She sprang back up, bouncing on her heels.

"No harm done," she said. "Off you go and pay your bill. Goodbye."

And she continued crossing the road, saved from further incident by the lack of oncoming traffic rather than by her following even basic safety precautions.

The driver of the car did not speak, shrug or get out of his car to inspect the slight dent to his bonnet. He remained stationary, with the engine running, until another car drove around the corner behind him and politely hooted. The slight and friendly parp-parp raised him from his reverie and he drove on.

And Bethany carried on walking, taking side-turns on a whim, doubling back if streets failed to meet her exacting standards, at one crossroads closing her eyes and spinning around and around faster and faster until she just couldn't stand the dizziness and the unsteadiness and the sheer uncertainty of it all and, at the moment when she just had to open her eyes, she kept them closed for the slightest moment longer and then started walking in the direction her nose was pointing and opened her eyes just to make sure she didn't walk into a brick wall or a lamp-post or an attractive man or a puzzled onlooker, of which there were only a handful and none of them were handsome.

When she heard a commotion on the street and she noticed people hurrying away, pretending they hadn't seen or heard, she ran, sprinting, head down, arms slicing the air, *towards* it.

The commotion was a shattering noise and some deep-voiced shouting and some higher-voiced fear and, as Bethany rounded the corner she saw the two men in motorcycle helmets and she saw the motorcycle and she saw the bars or sticks or machetes in their hands – it was so hard to tell which at this distance. And their hands that weren't holding sticks or machetes or iron bars were scrabbling around inside the jeweller's window and throwing whatever it was they were grabbing into a large holdall hanging from the motorcycle's handlebars.

The one on the left saw her coming – she knew this because he turned his head ever so slightly as she approached.

The one on the right was trying to untangle some trinket, no doubt of extreme cost if not worth, and was oblivious to her approach.

She had to get the timing just right. She hadn't tried a move like this since she was at school. She might have let the muscle tone slide. She might be carrying a few more pounds or ounces. She certainly wasn't wearing the right sort of shoes. She hadn't worn the right sort of shoes in years.

But she could make up for all those handicaps by using a surfeit of brio and panache, confidence and exuberance, bloody-mindedness and adrenaline.

She vaulted the pillion, landed squarely on the saddle, knocked the kickstand aside with her heel, twisted the throttle and was away, holdall bouncing back and forth onto the mudguard. She couldn't get the gear change right, the engine was roaring, and so she couldn't hear what chaos, disappointment, frustration, vengeance and application of justice were going on behind her. She just kept on going, cutting off the pavement onto the road eventually, hardly at the first opportunity, and continuing, engine no longer roaring but now screaming. She leaned backward a little and, much to her surprise and delight, the front wheel left the ground which made it so much easier to grab the holdall and swing it around onto her lap so that, when the wheel crashed back to tarmac, the journey felt more secure, less likely to end abruptly with a strap through the spokes and a high-speed hurtle across the handlebars.

But the engine noise was too loud for her and she was getting stares from passers-by and, probably, drivers – as much for her hair streaming backwards, not constrained by a helmet, as for the racket.

She stopped the motorcycle, parked it against a double-yellow line sporting three perpendicular no-loading stripes, zipped up the holdall and continued her walk.

And then she went into a post office.

She waited in the queue. It was short but slow-moving. People with two, three or fifteen parcels were weighing them, one after the other and the man behind her sighed and she turned around and looked the man up and down, her eyes taking in his once elegant jacket, now slightly fraying at the wrist, his once carefully pressed trousers now showing a double-crease around the knee and a few hem threads tickling the unevenly polished uppers of his shoes.

She smiled at him. He started and returned the smile unevenly.

"I'm Bethany," she said to him. "Do you think I can put this whole holdall in the post as it is?"

"I'm Victor," he said. "I don't see why not. Maybe seal it with parcel tape?"

"Good plan!" she said. "Keep my place, would you?" And, without waiting for a reply, she dropped the bag and began shuttling up and down the aisles, finally pouncing on a generously wide roll of brown tape.

"Would you hold the bag up for me?" she asked, returning to the queue.

"Certainly," said Victor.

He held the handles, she crouched and began to pick-pick-pick at the end of the roll. "The knees can't take it any more," she said, suddenly sitting on the floor and, without the ache, she found the end, pulled it away, stuck it to the bag and, with a most glorious tape-coming-off-a-roll sound, she wound tape around and around the bag, gradually making her way up its length, weaving it around the handles before pausing with only a couple of inches of bag still exposed.

"Better take something as a keepsake, I suppose," she said, unzipping the exposed two inches, reaching in and retrieving a gold (either colour or metal, she neither knew nor cared) man's watch and a similarly silver slender bracelet. "Ooh, one each," she said, passing the watch to Victor.

"I can't take this," he said.

"Suit yourself," she said, dropping it into her pocket. "Want to take the bracelet instead?"

"I don't think it would suit me," he said, frowning. "Is this some sort of prank? Are you a journalist? Do I recognise you from somewhere?"

"No," said Bethany, smiling. "Do journalists regularly try pranks on you?"

"Not as much as they used to," said Victor. He sighed.

"Did you used to be famous then?" asked Bethany.

"Yes," said Victor. "I'm still a little famous. Not

as much as I was. I thought I might get Oswald's job but, well, Duncan just didn't see it that way. Out of the frying pan and into the fridge. But never mind me. What's going on with this bag? It seems a little fishy to me."

"Oh don't you worry your little head about it, as my Nanna Doreen would have said," said Bethany. "But would you be a dear and send it for me? Any local police station will do."

"Not really," said Victor. "Firstly it'll cost a fortune and secondly I can't take a large bag full of goodness knows what from someone I don't know and put it in the post."

"Why can't you?" asked Bethany. "Why can't you have a little *trust*? The vast majority of people are honest, decent, hard-working, *charming* people. Change your mindset. Assume everyone you meet is going to be like that. Sure, you'll get ripped off or robbed or insulted or have your heart broken a few times in your life but think of that as a very small price for a much better life. Think about all the extra opportunities you'll have. And really – sending a holdall to the local nick isn't going to cost that much. Send it cash-on-delivery if you must."

"I know where I recognise you from!" said Victor. "You're the woman who walked out in front of my car this morning!"

"You mean you're the driver from the hit-and-run this morning?" said Bethany.

"But *you* hit *my* car," said Victor. "And *you* ran

away."

"Exactly," said Bethany. "Hit and run. That's what I said. And was there any harm done?"

"There's a dent in my bonnet," said Victor.

"All the best cars have dents in them," said Bethany. "It shows they've had an adventure. When did you last have an adventure?"

Victor didn't answer.

"So have one now!" said Bethany. "Maybe posting a parcel isn't much of an adventure – but think about where it might lead."

"I wouldn't expect posting someone else's parcel to lead anywhere for me and I'd rather not do it. Thank you for the opportunity but really all I need to do to have a charming day is to collect the seedlings that have been sent to this post office and go home and plant them and... Hey! Come back!"

Bethany had been stepping slowly backwards but then, in the middle of Victor's little speech she simply turned and walked briskly to the door and out into the street. He was, of course, still holding the bag.

She turned in the direction she hadn't come from and, without breaking step, she was away. A traffic warden was standing by the motorcycle, typing at the tiny keys of his handheld penalising machine.

Past the convenience store, turning left at the betting shop and lengthening her stride to cross the road before the traffic lights changed, she glanced at her watch. She nodded, mainly to herself, but caught the eye of the man with the large plastic bottle of glue, a small brush and a box of flyers.

He was just about to daub. She walked directly towards him, stopped a good few inches inside his personal space.

"How did it come to this?" she asked.

"Excuse me?" said the gluing man, retreating a half-step.

"Is this how you saw yourself twenty years ago when you left university?" she asked, shuffling forward a half-step.

"How did you know I went to university?" he asked.

"Just guessed," she said. "But you did – because if you hadn't you would have said so, rather than asking me how I knew. And only graduates from about twenty years ago would wear those sorts of trousers."

"They're just normal corduroy trousers!" he said, slightly louder, eyebrows set to faux indignity.

"I'm Bethany," she said, offering her hand which he failed to shake because his hands were full.

"Of course you are," he said. "I'm Adam."

"And are you slightly disappointed or do you run a group that stops slight disappointment from happening?" she asked, her gaze skittering across the pile of flyers neatly lying in the cardboard box.

"Both really," he said, smiling. "Do you want to come along to my group? We really got somewhere last week, really got through to someone, really got stuff done."

"Too many 'really's," she said. "Makes you sound desperate. It's basically a dating agency spun with a slightly unusual gloss to get damaged characters through the door. *Isn't it?*"

"No it isn't!" he said, the eyebrowed indignity shifting towards genuine.

"Yes it is," she said, but she said it *gently*, like she cared, and *softly*, like she sympathised and with a *half*-smile, like she maybe wasn't so far from needing the group herself.

"No it isn't," he said, but he was smiling this time, and his eyebrows were relaxed and he put down the box and the glue and the brush, and the brush went into the box and spoilt the top sheet with glue on the front and maybe some soaked further down the stack but he didn't look.

And now he held out his hand and she took it and finally they shook hands.

"Come with me," she said. "It's lucky I bumped into you. Everything will turn out just fine."

And she pulled his hand, but only gently, but he didn't resist and he tightened his grip and they started walking and it took about fifteen steps before he released her hand and took it again with his other hand so that he didn't have to walk with his arm crossed over his body. And they were holding hands as they walked along the road and both of them were fine with that and suddenly she turned left and opened a door and he followed her into the shop.

A man was sitting behind a table with three small piles of books arranged on one side. He had two pens neatly lined up in front of him. The walls of the shop were furnished, floor-to-ceiling, with bookcases, each shelf fully loaded with books. The body of the shop contained numerous tables displaying books in piles, on lean-stands or standing between brightly coloured bookends. There was a sign in front of the man with the pens. It matched the cover of the books piled on his table.

"A book signing?" asked Adam.

"Of course," said Bethany. "You should meet the author. Once he's finished with Bob."

"Who's Bob?" asked Adam.

"Oh, you wouldn't know him," said Bethany. "Loose end from the last book."

Another man, presumably Bob, was standing with his back to the door, talking across the table to the author. The author was sitting awkwardly in his seat, leaning firmly into the seat-back, as though trying to be as *far away* as possible, while Bob talked at him, hands vigorously annotating his words.

Bethany walked over and interrupted Bob's flow.

"Hello Bob," she said. "How's it going?"

"I'm not happy about this," said Bob. "I thought this business was finished for good last year. But you're right, Bethany. This is a better way to leave things."

"And so...?" said Bethany.

"I'm sorry about how things turned out," said Bob, turning to face the author but not quite looking him in the eye. His gaze found 'suspense and horror' on the shelf behind and held on tight. "I was just doing what I was told, following instructions, just my job, you know."

"I, er, well, it's partly my fault it, er, got the way it was. I mean, er, did," said the author.

"You sure you're an author, mate?" asked Bob. "Those words barely made a sentence."

"Bob!" said Bethany.

"Sorry," said Bob, glaring at her. "Just trying to lighten things up a bit. Anyway, no harm done?"

"Well, er, no lasting harm anyway," said the author. "Since you're here..." He gestured at the piles of books. The cover showed a grey day, all clouds, dreary sea and depressing beach with a garish child's sun scrawled over the top.

"Very kind of you," said Bob, picking up a copy. "Really feels like a proper book too." He flicked through the pages. "Crisp."

"You just need to pay at the till first," said the author, "then bring it back and I'll sign it for you."

Bob put the book down. "Not a gift then?" he asked.

"No," said the author.

"I'll wait for the film," said Bob. "But thanks for the chat. Good to finally, you know, *understand* my motivation." He fiddled with his ear and Adam noticed he was wearing a small earpiece with a curly wire disappearing into his clothing. "I probably won't see you again," he said to the author. Then he smiled. "In a good way," he said before turning, almost bumping into Adam, saying "Excuse me, sir," and leaving the shop before Adam could say, "Not at all" or "My fault" or attempt to apologise himself.

"Hello darling," said Bethany, leaning over the table and kissing the author.

"Hello Bethany," he said. "Who's this then? Dominic?"

"I'm Adam," said Adam. "How do you do?"

"I was hoping for Dominic," said the author, ignoring Adam.

"I tried," said Bethany. "He couldn't think outside his own story. Ended up settling the bill with Janice and..."

"Who's Janice?" asked the author.

"Coffee shop waitress," said Bethany.

"You got the wrong Dominic," said the author. "I wanted palm reader Dominic. The one with the beard."

"He *had* a beard. I went where you told me to go," said Bethany. "I saw the number six bus pull away and there he was and..."

"And?"

"And there *was* another man a few hundred yards further up the road."

"Excuse me," said Adam, "I know a Dominic. He

comes to my group. Is that who you're trying to find? Because we're meeting tomorrow and I can..."

"Different person," said the author.

"But he could be the person Bethany met," said Adam.

"He could," said the author. He cleared his throat. "Adam, thank you for coming but I don't really have anything to tell you."

"I didn't come here to speak to you," said Adam. "I came because Bethany asked and, well, she's quite charming."

"Isn't she?" said the author, grinning.

"You do know I can hear you?" said Bethany. "I thought Adam was on the list."

"Second tier," said the author. "He knows who he is and what he's doing. It's a slow start but it's rewarding and I don't think he needs any explanations."

"Explanations?" said Adam.

"I asked Bethany to round up some of the characters," said the author. "You know, tidy things up a little, deal with any loose ends and give me a chance to see how they've got on since."

"Since you're talking about loose ends," said Bethany, "what was the jewellery shop robbery all about?"

"Just a tangent," said the author. "A little interlude between Victor running into you and you running into him. I thought you might enjoy it. Did you?"

"Yes," said Bethany, smiling. "Thank you."

"You're welcome," said the author. He smiled too. They shared a moment.

"Has Ed been in yet?" asked Bethany, breaking the silence, moving the story along.

"Yes," said the author. "He brought his photos. Even I couldn't tell they weren't genuine and I came up with the idea. He seemed..."

"Yes?" asked Bethany.

"He seemed healthy," said the author. "Relaxed." He paused. "Speaking of photos, Justin sent me a few photos from the wedding – Ina looking strikingly beautiful, Kosta looking dapper and delighted, the church looking, well, *churchy* by the sea with the sunlight glinting..."

"Is that a tear in the corner of your eye?" asked Bethany.

"I have been known to be overly sentimental," said the author. He coughed, cleared his throat and made other clichéd noises normally associated with being caught while being overly sentimental. "Anyway, they won't be in because they're still on their honeymoon. But I do hope you managed to find..."

"No," said Bethany. "You won't get *her* here."

"Who?" asked the author.

"You know," said Bethany. "Before her relaunch, maybe she would have been tempted. But now she's on tour..."

"On tour?" asked the author. "Big venues?"

"Clearly," said Bethany. "But don't get excited. It's not *her* tour. She's joining *him* on stage for a couple of songs. And no, they're not currently in the country. And also, no, even if they were in the country, you wouldn't get *him* along here, although she *might* have come out of curiosity."

The author looked briefly downhearted. But then a thought occurred to him. "How about...?" he asked.

"I'm pretty sure he'll be along," said Bethany.

"Are you now?" said Victor. He had arrived during the conversation about Ruth's world tour although he had had little idea what they were talking about. Even if they had mentioned names, he would probably still have been none the wiser. Curiously, from where Bethany was standing, Victor appeared to be underneath the dangling sign for the true-crime section, almost as though it was pointing at him.

"Not you," said Bethany. "But have a chat as you're here."

"This won't take long either," said the author. "Hello Victor. No, I don't mind about Oswald. Yes, you are going to get away with it. No, he doesn't get a happy ending because that would give many millions of other people a very *unhappy* ending. So, on balance, in your story, everything turns out just fine."

"Sorry, who are you?" asked Victor.

"Have a copy," said the author. "No charge. I'll

sign it for you if you like."

"Thank you," said Victor. "What's it about?"

"About a couple of hundred pages," said the author, wincing at his own quip. "Sorry. And it's not even original. The book is, though." He signed inside the cover, blew on the ink then handed the book to Victor.

"Oh, Bethany?" said Victor, ignoring the joke but taking the book, "I took your bag to the police. The man in the post office told me it was only a couple of hundred yards down the road so it seemed easier to carry it than to post it."

"Were they pleased to see it?" asked Bethany.

"Not really, I..." said Victor.

"I don't think we need to turn this into a police procedural," said the author. "But tell me – what brought you in here today?"

"She slipped this into my pocket," said Victor, pulling out a crumpled piece of paper with the name and address of the bookshop written hastily and messily across it. "An unusual invitation, admittedly, but it didn't seem risky to come here. And I'm a big supporter of independent bookshops."

"And I'm a big supporter of independent authors," said Gabriel, "especially authors who go out of their way to get my attention."

Gabriel paused, standing artistically framed in the doorway, sunlight slanting past him, leaving him in shadow, an ineffective attempt at a big entrance for a man neither expected by his audience nor likely to have been recognised by most of them – even if they had been able to make out his face.

Bethany recognised him and walked to the other side of the nearest bookcase. Her face was now framed by the signs for 'true-crime' and 'motor-sports'. Admittedly those sections were unlikely to be placed together in a normal shop but artistic licence allows for satisfying arrangements in fiction. After all, if the fourth wall is to come down, it might as well come down *really* hard.

"Oh really?" said the author.

"Yes really," said Gabriel. "The policeman asked whether I was still going to make it to my book signing and I said I didn't have one today and he said that was funny because he'd found a flyer in the glove compartment when he'd recovered the car. He sounded a bit disappointed, like I was being disrespectful to his detective work."

"Hardly detective work to open a glove compartment and have a look," said the author.

"Indeed," said Gabriel. "If he'd bothered to read beyond the words 'book' and 'signing', he might have noticed your name instead of mine. As he did when I asked him to read the rest of it to me. So here I am."

"Thank you for coming," said the author.

"Pleasure," said Gabriel. "So, is this book as good as the last one?"

"Of course," said the author.

"In that case, I'll handle the marketing budget, pre-order a couple of hundred-thousand so you've got something to live off and take my usual percentage. Shall I have my people put it in writing and send it to your people?"

"I am my own people," said the author. "But other than that, yes, please, by all means, thank you."

"You're welcome," said Gabriel.

"Do you know, dear reader," said the author, before dispensing with the quotation marks, I think everything will turn out just fine.